CROSSING OVER

OVER

PAUL CLAYTON

Crossing Over
Copyright © 2018 by Paul Clayton. All rights reserved.
First Edition

Cover and Formatting: Streetlight Graphics

To Stephen Gallup, friend and editor, author of *What About the Boy?* and James N. Frey, friend and mentor, author of *How to Write a Damn Good Novel*

I

Mɪᴋᴇ McNᴇʀɴᴇʏ's ᴡɪꜰᴇ ᴅɪᴅ ɴᴏᴛ like the idea of him going, but he had insisted, wanting to witness firsthand what happened at these, almost-daily, political protests. He turned the volume on the AM radio in the truck all the way up as he drove. The signal was weak; the station was rogue, over a hundred miles away, changing location daily. Three months earlier, the New York, New Jersey, Pennsylvania, Connecticut, Massachusetts, and Maine State Guard units had formed a bloc, the Liberty League, loosely aligning themselves with the radical Revolutionary Peoples' Party, the RPP. They favored the government of the newly declared president. Then, West Virginia, Tennessee, Kentucky, North and South Carolina, Alabama, Georgia and some counties in Virginia, combined their State Guard units, called themselves the Minute Men, and declared allegiance to the recently-ousted president and national government in exile.

As Mike came into the outskirts of town, he passed the North Side shopping center. He turned on Main and was surprised to see a light through the tinted glass of the long-closed Atlas Hardware. He drove past and saw one of the front glass doors off the hinges and lying on the pavement. A small fire burned in the center of the building with a few individuals moving about it... transients and homeless. Hopefully, the authorities would roust them soon.

He parked a block from the town center and locked the truck. Walking slowly toward the square, he was surprised at how few pedestrians he saw. The gravel lot where the Provident Bank once stood was usually filled with Flea Market vendors and shoppers. Now it was empty, perhaps in anticipation of trouble. Turning the corner, he could hear drumming and a protest chant of some kind. He saw a small crowd of about thirty or so people near the fountain. He approached, watching them milling about—mostly white, with a few blacks and Hispanics. Surprisingly, about a quarter of them were female. All of them looked to be in their twenties or thirties. They wore dark clothing and carried backpacks. Many wore hoodies and had bandanas around their necks that could be pulled up to hide their faces.

Before the government had shut down the TV

stations, Mike had watched a couple of protests, but the footage was always severely edited, and you could never tell what really happened. Everything in the country, from cuisine to music, even the weather, had become hyper-political and vehemently argued over. Simple truth, so-called common sense and values, and dialogue had died in the last five or so years.

"They're coming," announced a big, tough-looking young woman pointing south on Federal Street.

Mike turned and saw the protestors, about a dozen of them, mostly middle-aged people, walking slowly toward them carrying flags and placarded signs.

The counter-protestors formed up into a loose group and a middle-aged man with a full beard, evidently their leader, addressed them in low tones that Mike could not decipher. Finishing, he led the group closer to Federal Street. The protestors began filing by, looking over in surprise at the crowd gathered to watch them.

They chanted as they walked, "God and Freedom, U-S-A, everyone must have their say!"

Someone among the town counter-protestors threw a rock, striking a man on the arm. He looked up worriedly but continued to march slowly behind the others.

"Go back where you belong, Fucktards!" a young, male counter-protestor shouted.

Mike watched in fascination, then looked around, wondering where the police were. He thought he saw a squad car a block away, but it appeared to be parked. He saw no police officers. He returned his gaze to the marchers. One woman's sign proclaimed, LEAVE MY PRESIDENT ALONE!

"Get the fuck out of here, Granny," shouted one of the hooded young men, "before you get your ass kicked!"

Mike's face was pinched with concern for the little group marching through, and anger toward them as well, for having put themselves at risk.

Most of the marchers passed the crowd of counter-protestors without incident. A man in his mid-fifties brought up the rear. He had fallen slightly behind. FREE SPEECH, his sign proclaimed, USE IT, OR LOSE IT. He looked up at the bearded leader of the counter protestors and paused. "You're old enough to know what's at stake here," he shouted. "Why don't you join us?"

The counter-protestors began chanting,

"Racist, fascist, homophobe, we're gonna pound you in the road."

Undeterred, the man shouted up, "Tell them to stand down. You know better. Join us."

The bearded leader ignored him, turning, and walking away.

Mike did not want to get involved but felt compelled to shout at the protestor. "What good is this doing? This isn't going to change anyone's mind. You'll just stir things up."

The man's eyes found Mike's. "Doesn't matter," he said. "Freedom, brother... Use it or lose it!"

Mike said nothing further. The sign-holding man turned and saw that his fellow protestors had moved on. He started walking to catch up, but the counter-protestors quickly surrounded him. Mike followed along at the edge of the crowd.

The man looked around at the crowd. His stern look was crumbling, turning to one of fear. "What is it about free speech that scares you people?" he said shrilly.

The crowd drew closer around him, mere feet away.

A short, stocky man wearing a black, watch

cap pushed to the fore. "You mean 'hate speech,'" he said, "don't you, motherfucker?"

"No. I mean free speech."

"Fuck you, racist!" screamed one of the women, "we know what you mean!"

Mike felt the electric tension rising. All eyes were on the man with the sign. Mike looked back again to see where the police were. There weren't any.

The counter-protestor in the watch cap stepped right up into the protestor's face. "Hate speech ain't free, motherfucker," he said. "There's a price."

Before the protestor could answer the man in the cap sucker punched him full in the face. Blood gushed from his nose and he dropped his sign. The other counter-protestors began pummeling him from every direction, knocking him to the ground.

"Stop!" shouted Mike. "Wait!"

Shouts and cries from the victim's fellow protestors came from the distance as they began making their way back.

The counter-protestors continued to kick and stomp the man as he rolled about, attempting to protect his body. A young man built like a football player ran forward and kicked the man's head—a punter going for a field goal. The man stopped moving. Emboldened, others on the fringe of the crowd ran forward to quickly stomp on the man's inert form and dance away in mock fright. Several men from both groups now faced off and traded blows as some of the protestors knelt to the unconscious man. Feeling numb, Mike turned away and walked back in the direction of his truck.

II

MIKE LISTENED TO THE RADIO in the kitchen as he made a pot of coffee. He hoped to hear more about the fighting, how close things were getting. He had a family to protect. His wife, Marie, hardly ever listened to the news. It upset her too much. One of them had to know what was going on.

He leaned toward the radio, straining to hear the broadcaster's voice over the static. The news was not good: A Pennsylvania Air National Guard jet had just been shot down over the Pennsylvania/Maryland border. The Liberty League was now promising to shoot down two of the Minute Men's planes for every one they lost. A food riot in Philly had turned racial, with people being hunted down by mobs and beaten to death. In Minneapolis, the two sides had recently squared off against each other at an RPP rally. That was only a hundred and fifty miles away. And, of course, there was the rally in town the day before that he had witnessed. He would have to talk with Marie about making serious plans to get him, her and their daughter, Elly, to a safer place. Some of the people in the neighborhood had already moved north to the countryside.

As Mike listened, he became aware of Marie's steps on the stairs. He turned and smiled as she entered the kitchen. "Just in time," he said.

Marie frowned at the droning radio. "Do we have to have that on all the time?"

He clicked it off. "Not all the time, but there are some new, concerning reports."

"What happened at that protest you went to yesterday?" she said.

Mike blinked thoughtfully. "Not much. Just two bunches of people shouting at each other for a while."

"Carol came by after dinner last night when you were working in the back yard. She said a man was severely injured and is in a coma."

"Well, there was some fighting, but I didn't want to upset you. I didn't know anyone got hurt that bad."

Marie shook her head. "It's awful."

The coffee machine beeped, and Mike smiled sadly. "The coffee's ready."

She came to him and put her arm around him. "Not too strong, I hope."

He shook his head. "Just the way you like it." He pulled her close and kissed her. She responded and they both felt an awakening of passion. "I wish we would have done that last night," he said. "Could have been the start of something."

She looked up into his eyes. "I know. It's just that I'm so tired lately with everything that's happening. And when I finally do manage to fall asleep, it's not very good."

"That's okay," he said, kissing her again. "I understand." Their kisses went deeper. Through half-closed eyelids Mike saw Elly come into the room and burst out in bright laughter, saying, "Kissy face, kissy face."

Mike and Marie laughed uncomfortably.

"Okay," said Marie, "enough of that. C'mon, Elly. Help me set the table."

Mike smiled as he watched Elly take the cups out of the cupboard. He could not help taking stock of her as she set them on the table. She was already an inch taller than her mother, and at sixteen, she likely had more growing to do. She had the body and face of a teen model, and the mind of a child of eleven or twelve. Normally of good temper, she was the source of much joy and wonderment for Mike and Marie, but also worry.

Her beauty turned heads wherever they went, especially male heads.

Mike sat and dropped two tablets of saccharin into his coffee. He stirred it, watching it fizz faintly white, his mind clouding over in thought. You couldn't get sugar anymore, nor honey. They hadn't seen either in over six months.

Marie shook some government-rationed corn flakes from a brown cardboard box into Elly's bowl and her own, then poured over it some canned milk she had cut with water.

Elly opened the sugar bowl and stuck her spoon in, digging about. "Aw," she crooned childishly, "still no sugar?"

Marie looked over her coffee cup. "Sorry."

"No honey either?" said Elly, as if Mike and Marie were holding out on her.

"No," said Marie. "You want to go shopping with me today after your lessons? Maybe we can find some."

"Yeah, Mommy," she said, her tone brighter.

Mike smiled benignly. Such exchanges were their norm and of no note. But when they went out, Elly's childlike behavior elicited inquisitive looks and smiles. There had always been hints that she would have deficits, but the retardation had become undeniable when she was six and in school. She could not keep up with the other kids. They put her in Special Ed and that had helped. But her most worrisome trait became evident when she would play in the front yard or on the street in front of the house. She was overly friendly with the neighbors, stopping them to talk. And she had a total lack of fear of strangers, often calling out to them when she was riding her bike on the street. Mike's heart ached as he recalled his little girl at twelve or so, her breasts already budding, her hips developing, sitting on her bicycle under her Disney Aladdin helmet, calling out to the occasional stranger walking by while Mike watched protectively from in front of the house. Once he had had to pursue Elly as she followed an older man who was walking his dog down the street. When Mike caught up to them, she turned and said, "He's going to let me walk his dog."

Mike stared at the man angrily.

"I never told her that," the stranger protested, "I just told her I'd think about it."

Marie broke into his thoughts. "It's nice out today."

He nodded and glanced out the window.

"Yeah. But the temperature is supposed to drop down to the forties tonight. Winter's on its way."

"That's good," said Elly. "Maybe it will snow." She looked brightly at her father. "If it snows can you help me make a snowman?"

Mike and Marie laughed.

"Of course," said Mike. "Maybe you could start getting the stuff we'll need ready, like gloves, buttons for eyes and nose ... coal."

"Yeah," said Elly with wonder. She frowned as she placed her spoon in her bowl and pushed it to the center of the table. "I wonder where Charley is. I miss him."

Mike wondered too. Their little border collie had been missing for three days. Other dogs had probably killed him. With the food shortages and pet-abandonments, there were packs of feral dogs running around. "Well," he said, trying to sound hopeful, even though he wasn't, "maybe he'll show up today."

"All right, Elly," said Marie. "We'll look for him later. Now you can help me clean up."

"Okay, Mommy."

Marie put Elly to work folding the laundry she'd brought in off the clothesline. She thought of the relatively new dryer they had, but rarely used, due to the price of natural gas. Still, they were better off than a lot of folks, given the news reports and the stories told by the neighbors about the strangers passing through town. And there was something fulfilling about the added chores they had now. They brought them together as a family.

Marie went out to the backyard and took down the supports for the tomatoes and beans that they had grown and canned. She bundled up the stakes and laid them by the door for Mike to put away in the shed. She thought of their embrace in the kitchen before Elly interrupted them. Mike was right. They had not made love in a while, maybe three weeks. And they'd had opportunities. But what she told him was true; she was often just too tired. It wasn't the extra work; it was the worry. She could not understand how people could let their differences come to a head like this. It boiled down to a lack of leadership at the top on both sides.

Sighing, she looked at the empty house next door and wondered about Charley. Elly missed him a lot. She headed for the detached garage.

Maybe Charley had holed up in there for some reason.

The light was muted, the air musty. She walked the length of the truck camper to the roll-up door, looking under the shelves. A plastic bin hid most of a darkened space and she tugged on it, sliding it out scratchily. She heard the sound of fabric sliding off something and stood. A set of intense, angry eyes under a hooded face fixed on her as a wild-looking young man sat up.

Mike was in the back shed getting his work gloves and equipment. On the radio the week before he had heard that there would be natural gas shortages this winter and he had decided to cut down one of the two maple trees in the back yard for firewood. He was lifting an axe off the shelf when Marie screamed from the direction of the garage. He bounded out the door, axe in hand.

The back door to the garage was open as Mike ran in. Marie stood between the Ford camper and the long work bench. She had evidently surprised someone sleeping on top of the workbench. A thuggish-looking white kid wearing a hooded sweatshirt zipped halfway down, tattoos up to his jawline, slid off the bench as Mike came up.

"What the hell are you doing in here?" Mike demanded. For a moment he thought he saw cunning in the youth's eyes, then hurt. The smoky grey eyes slid smoothly from Mike's face to Marie's.

"Sorry, man. I just needed a place to rest. I'll be going, okay?"

"He didn't do anything," said Marie. "I was looking for Charley and when I thought I saw something behind the trash bin, I pulled it out to get a closer look." She looked at Mike. "And he sat up and that's what scared me."

Mike stared at the teen. He had a sparse fuzzy beard and acne on his cheeks. He did not seem particularly strong or threatening, but there had been reports of teen thugs travelling in gangs. Mike recalled the squatters around their fire inside the Atlas Hardware. This one probably had friends around somewhere.

"Yeah," said Mike, "well, he can't stay in here. I'll see him to the gate."

The teen straightened up and blinked the sleep out of his eyes. He was a couple inches taller than Mike. His pants were, of course, sagging. He was lean but muscled. He rubbed the slight hollow of his stomach lazily. "Y'all got any food? I ain't had nothin' to eat in a day."

Mike wanted to trust him, but nowadays you could not trust anybody you did not know, and he wanted him gone. "Look," he said. "There's a food bank down at the Court House. They'll feed you. But you can't hang around here."

Marie's voice was tinged with concern. "Mike, we can at least give him something to take with him. I'll go put some food in a plastic bag."

Mike didn't like the idea but shrugged. "All right."

Marie hurried back to the house.

Mike looked at the teen. "You can wait out by the gate. We'll get you something to take with you."

The teen blinked and nodded eagerly. "Thanks, man. That's cool. I just wanna eat, you understand. Then I'm outta here."

Mike left the teen at the gate. He went back inside the house, shut the front door, and locked it. He quickly went upstairs to the bedroom and opened the safe, taking out the thirty-eight police special. He didn't particularly like guns. In fact, he had long believed there should be more legal restrictions against them. But when the country's political problems began to escalate to street violence, he decided he had better have one to protect his family. He had only fired the thing once at an indoor range. Marie did not like him having it in the house and so he had bought the safe for it. He never intended to carry it around and didn't have a holster for it. He had hoped he could just leave it in the safe forever. But now he could not shake a premonition of vulnerability. He opened the cylinder; five brass shell casings shone in the dull light. He closed it carefully and put it in his pocket.

Mike started down the stairs. Before he could shout, he watched in disbelief as Elly opened the front door to the teen thug and stepped back. Marie was approaching and the teen grabbed her, putting her in a head lock; she dropped the sack of food. The teen pulled out a stiletto knife and held it to her throat. Elly whimpered and ran into the living room. "I'm sorry, Mommy," she called out repeatedly.

The teen saw Mike hurrying down the stairs and shielded himself with Marie. He pushed further into the house and kicked the door closed behind him, keeping the knife pressed to Marie's throat. He glared up at Mike, "Listen, motherfucker, all I want is the keys to the camper. Gimme the fuckin' keys and I'm gone, you understand?"

Mike stepped onto the landing; he was only seven or eight feet away. He knew there could be no negotiating, no backing down. Now it was the keys to the camper he wanted. Then what? Mike took the revolver from his pocket and aimed it at the teen's head. "Let her go," he said. "Do it or I'll kill you."

Marie's face was a mask of fear. She closed her eyes and said nothing. The thug tried to scrunch down, making himself less of a target, but ended up pulling Marie lower. He straightened up a bit. "Oh, shit!" he said with mock bravado, "You ain't kidding, are you?"

Mike did not say anything, trying instead to slow his breathing. He steadied his right wrist with his left hand, sighting along the little barrel at the thug's head. His vision blurred slightly. His glasses had moved, but he did not dare touch them. He continued to sight along the barrel. He was only five or so feet away. He couldn't miss, he kept telling himself.

"All right, man, okay. Don't shoot." The thug lowered the knife and slipped it into his pocket, backing away from Marie who appeared ready to faint.

"Marie," said Mike, "go in the other room."

Marie hurried into the living room and Mike moved closer to the thug. "Now get out."

Mike was behind him when he spun around, throwing Mike off balance. One of his hands was on the revolver, the other gripped Mike's shirt. Mike pushed him back and, in the process, squeezed the trigger. The revolver exploded percussively. Mike felt the recoil. He could not hear. He saw movement and turned—Elly racing up the stairs in panic. His hearing came back in a burst—Marie to his left, screaming at him, the thug leaning against the door, moaning as he held his hand aloft, blood dripping down his arm.

Mike pushed him sideways and jerked the door open. He gave him a shove. The thug stood on the stoop, his eyes half-open in pain and disbelief. Mike aimed the revolver at his face. "Get out! Get the fuck out of here!"

"I'm going, man, don't shoot." The thug held his bloody hand aloft. He turned to stare angrily at Mike as he walked down the walkway. Mike followed at a distance. A black man wearing a navy-blue jacket and hoody walked up to the gate. He looked at the thug, then at Mike. "What the fuck?" he said.

The teen thug waved his bleeding hand, glaring at Mike. "We'll get your ass, motherfucker. We'll be back."

Mike brought the weapon up again and sighted carefully along the snub barrel. "Get out of here."

"Shit!" hissed the black man. They turned and went down the street.

Mike waited on his walkway for a few minutes. He walked to the gate and looked around. They had disappeared somewhere. He pocketed the revolver and went back into the house. He locked the door and proceeded into the living room. Marie sat on the couch, her face wet with tears.

Mike sat beside her, one ear attuned to the doors and windows. "Marie …"

She said nothing, not turning to him.

"I'm sorry, Honey. I didn't mean to scare you."

"You shot him!"

"Yeah!" Mike sighed in frustration. "The gun went off. He was trying to take it from me."

She turned to him angrily. "You could've shot me!"

The vehemence in her voice shocked him.

"Damn it, Marie, I wouldn't do that! I had to get him out of here, okay? I had to scare him away."

They heard Elly crying upstairs. She always ran away when they fought, racing to her room, slamming the door, and throwing herself across her bed. This time she had good cause.

Marie buried her face in her hands and sobbed. "I was so scared. No one's ever pointed a gun at me. Ever!"

Mike was flailing desperately for the right words, like a drowning man grabbing at water. "C'mon, Marie, what the hell could I do? If I had given him the keys to the camper you think he would have just left?"

Marie said nothing, continuing to sob.

"If I hadn't done what I did he would be in here now, maybe with his friends. Don't you understand? One of his friends met him at the gate." Mike shook his head in frustration. Marie just didn't understand how bad things had become. She did not have the big picture of what was happening all around them, what was coming. Society was in a slow-motion collapse. They had to be pro-active now.

Mike tried again. "Marie," he said more gently, "he wouldn't have left." Mike looked up the stairs to see if Elly was watching them; she was not. He turned back to Marie. "He could've brought in his friends, okay? He's probably got more than one. Who knows what would've happened?"

Marie took her hands away from her face. She wiped the tears away from her eyes with a tissue. "What are we going to do?"

Mike surprised himself with his answer. "We're gonna get the hell out of here. There are reports of fighting over in Minneapolis, gangs of people coming through, and this thug will come back with his friends. We have to go!"

Marie's face was vacant.

Mike continued, "Ed Brock told me that the Fergusons already moved out."

She looked at him. "Really?"

"Yeah. They're headed for Canada. Other people are talking about it too."

"Do you think we'd be safe there?"

Mike put his arm around her. "Yeah, safer than here."

"I'll have to start packing."

They sat quietly for a few moments.

Mike kissed her forehead. "I'm sorry, Hon. I didn't mean to frighten you. Really. I'm sorry."

"It's okay." Marie sniffed. "I better go up and see how Elly's doing." She got to her feet.

Mike stood. "Okay. Look. I'm going across the street to check on the Turners. I'll lock the door. Don't go out. I'll be right across the street and I won't be gone more than a couple minutes. Then we'll start packing the camper."

Marie nodded sadly and went up the stairs.

Mike walked out into the middle of the street, his hand on the revolver in his pocket. He looked around. He did not see anyone. He went in the Turner's gate and knocked on their door. No one answered. He tried the handle; it was locked. He peered into their garage and saw that their van was gone. They must have left in the night. He went back to the door and looked through the window. Seeing nothing suspicious, he went to the house next door and found Ed and Carol Brock in their driveway, packing up their Toyota with gallon bottles of water, small cartons packed with boxes of spaghetti and noodles, canned vegetables and fruit, sardines, tuna fish, Spam.

Carol grimaced as he told her about finding the teen thug at his place. He omitted the part about shooting him in the hand. Ed continued to go and come from the house with cartons and bags. After filling the trunk, he closed it and turned to Mike.

"There were three of them in the Turners' last night. They must have broken in the back. I kept our lights out and fortunately they never tried to get in our place."

Carol took Ed's arm.

Ed shook his head as he looked at Mike. "We're not spending another night here, Mike. We're going up to Michigan. You should get your family out too. This place is too dangerous."

Mike nodded, mentally counting the families left in the cul-de-sac: his, Ron and Cindy Simmons, and the Brocks. And now they were getting out.

"I know," said Mike. "We're getting ready today. We'll probably leave sometime tomorrow."

Ed started back toward the house, his face set with concern. He paused. "You'd better not wait too long. There's nobody left to help us anymore." He went in his side door.

Carol hugged Mike. "Good luck," she said, her eyes misting up. "Tell Marie you'll all be in my prayers." She opened the back door of the Toyota and unfolded a blanket onto the seat.

Mike and Marie made a big meal of the

perishables in the refrigerator. After Elly went to bed they sat quietly at the table.

Mike looked out the window. "We have about another three hours of light. We should get packed up before it gets dark and then lock ourselves in for the night."

"Okay," said Marie. "I'll pack Elly's things. You can pack ours. We can both pack the clothes."

Later Mike jammed a couple dozen cardboard boxes as snugly as he could under the camper's sleeping shelves and table.

Marie came into the camper with the last box of Elly's things. "There's something upstairs I want to show you," she said.

"Okay."

Mike followed her into the spare bedroom. Elly's crib, playpen and highchair were arranged in the middle of the floor. Marie said nothing as she looked at him.

He smiled sadly. "We can't, Marie. We just don't have the room."

"Can't we fit them on half of our bed or something?"

He put his arm around her and pulled her to him. "We don't need those things anymore."

She laid her head against his chest. "Somebody might."

"Maybe. But we're going to be living in that camper. We need the space."

"You're right," she said.

"I wish I wasn't."

"I know."

Mike kissed her and they turned off the light, closed the door, and went downstairs. Marie slept on the couch and Mike on the floor with the revolver heavy and reassuring in his pocket. They left the next morning. As Mike approached the Atlas Hardware to turn onto the main road, he saw the thug and his black friend. They stood talking to another transient. Two beat-up Honda dirt bikes leaned on their stands nearby. The thug noticed the camper and said something to the others. They turned to stare angrily.

The thug waved his up-raised, bandaged hand, yelling at Mike, "Your house is ours, motherfucker!"

Mike pressed down hard on the gas. He looked at Marie, but she did not appear to have heard what he said.

III

MIKE SLOWLY MANEUVERED THE FORD pickup through the ruts and mud puddles of the sandy road as the day waned.

"Do you think they're following us?" said Marie. "On their motorcycles?"

"No. Those bikes were small, maybe 150 cc engines. I don't think they could keep up with us. They're probably ransacking our house instead."

Marie put her hand over her eyes and said nothing.

Broad pillars of pale winter light fell gently down through the trees as the truck creaked and swayed due to the high camper in its bed. A laugh came from inside the camper—Elly, enjoying the rocking of the rig and the sound of the occasional drooping tree branch whisking along the fiberglass roof. Mike had wanted Elly up front with them so they could talk to her before they set up for the night. He had wanted to go over their camping rules again about whom she could talk to, and when, whom she could not, and most importantly, never to be out of sight of the camper and her mother and father. But Marie had given into Elly's pleas to be allowed to ride in the back and listen to her music and fuss with her dolls. And with all that was happening, Marie was stressed enough. Why push it? He frowned in concentration, his hands gripping the wheel tightly. They needed each other more than ever now if they were going to get into Canada.

Another girlish giggle erupted from the back. Mike smiled sadly and turned to see if Marie would react. She did not. Mike guided the truck another mile down the muddy, rutted road and caught sight of some cars and campers a quarter mile ahead. He pulled to the side of the road to assess the situation.

"You're not going in?" said Marie, coming out of her fog.

"Not yet. We'll go in. But I just want to check the place out from a distance for a minute or two."

Marie said nothing. A year ago, she would have objected. She would have accused him of being paranoid and anti-social and would have insisted they park in the midst of the others and be sociable. But everything had changed. On the East Coast it had not taken long for the thin veneer of civilization to come unglued. People were less trusting, and for good reason; petty crime was commonplace, and ignored; violent crime had ratcheted way up as packs of transients roamed the freeways, coming through the towns to take what they could. Bands of home-grown vigilantes had sprung up. They were inexperienced and heavy-handed, and the justice they dished out was left hanging where all could see, until the dwindling numbers of moralists and Christian do-gooders took them down. Government troops did their best, but they often did not arrive until after the troublemakers had moved on. Once the troops established themselves, conditions stabilized to a basic level of civilization. Government script became available in the ATMs, twenty dollars per person per day, bulk food— flour, dried beans, rice, coffee, tea, canned milk, macaroni—at the local municipal building. People home-schooled their children. Deaths due to diseases and medical shortages became commonplace, especially among the elderly. Mental illness and suicides skyrocketed. And when the civil war had reached Chicago, it was not long after that the thug had shown up in their garage.

Mike and Marie sat in the cab of the truck

watching the camp as the engine ticked the seconds off. It seemed normal and safe. Mike again began slowly driving down the rutted road. Turning into the entrance, he pulled off onto a short, expanse of shoulder just past the gates. He set the parking brake and left the engine running. They looked around. A column of grey smoke rose from beyond the nearest row of campers, but they saw no people about.

"Kind of quiet," said Marie.

"Yeah. Probably most of them have been driving all night and half the day, just like us. What do you say we just stay here on the outskirts? We're only staying the night anyway. If we get up and get moving early, we can make the border by tomorrow night."

"All right," she said.

Mike turned the engine off. He sat for a moment, his hand resting on the hard outline of the .38 in his pocket. Marie did not know he carried it all the time now, and he had decided to keep it that way. The thug in the garage had brought reality home. If you owned a gun but didn't have it on you when you needed it, what good was it? You were prey and that was all there was to it.

He and Marie got out of the truck. He decided not to set the stabilizers in case they had to leave in a hurry. Going around to the back of the camper, he called, "Elly, time to come out."

"But I'm not finished."

Mike opened the back door. Elly was reaching into her little, portable doll house, which sat on the dinette table.

"You have to help your mom, okay?"

"Okay, Daddy."

Mike left the door open. Marie began untying the folding camp chairs and table from the rack on the back of the camper.

"I'm going to take a look around the camp," he said. "I'll be back in about ten minutes or so."

Marie nodded. "Okay. I'll be getting things ready for dinner."

Mike walked off. Between the first and second rows of campers he saw only one old couple sitting out in lawn chairs. They waved as he went past. He found more life further in, one big clan of travelers, probably extended family and neighbors, sitting around a big fire that was sending up the plume of smoke he had spotted earlier. An old man was strumming a guitar and singing an old folk song in a weak voice as Mike walked past.

"Where you from?" someone called to him.

Mike turned to see a man about his own age. "Near La Crosse," he said, "headed up to Canada."

"What's happening down there?"

"Shortages, food and fuel, lots of transients coming through."

The man nodded. "Yeah, I know. You mean thieves and thugs. We're going to our place up near the border, off in the woods. A big spread. About five families will be settling there."

"Any news?" said Mike.

The man shook his head slightly. "Just what we hear on the AM radio ... skirmishes, peace feelers, more skirmishes. The main event ain't started yet."

Mike nodded and moved off. He walked the equivalent of two blocks to the end of the camp, turned and started back on the other side. He was almost to the end when he saw Elly and a boy about her age leaving the camp and walking along a footpath that led into the woods. He hurried up to them.

"Elly? Where are you going?"

She and the boy turned. The boy's face was composed, innocent, but Mike wasn't buying it.

Elly's face was devoid of guilt or concern. "We're going to see some kittens, Daddy. Josh knows where they are."

"Did you ask Mommy?"

"No-oh," Elly said slowly with childlike, mock coyness. "We're not going far, Daddy."

"I don't care. You're not supposed to go off by yourself. C'mon. We're going back."

The boy's face darkened in annoyance, but he said nothing.

"Sorry," Elly said to him. "I can't go."

The boy frowned and said nothing. He walked off.

After they were out of earshot of the boy Mike said, "You know you're supposed to ask before you go off like that."

"Sorry, Daddy. He's a nice boy."

"It doesn't matter." They came into view of their camper. "Those are the rules."

"Okay." Elly said nothing further, not wanting her mother to know.

Marie had set up the aluminum table and chairs and was going through the picnic cooler as they walked up.

"What's for dinner?" said Mike.

Marie did not look up. Mike could tell by the look on her face that she knew something had happened and would bring it up with him later. "Well," she said, "hamburgers, some beans out of the can."

"Hamburgers again?" said Elly.

"Who in the world doesn't like hamburgers," said Mike with a forced laugh. "I'll get some firewood and get a fire going."

Mike and Marie made small talk, enjoying the pink sunset clouds of early evening as they sat close to the campfire. Elly had her earphones on, listening to one of her CDs. The people camped across from them were quiet, with only an occasional laugh or coughing spell reaching them.

Later Mike and Marie lay quietly in the double bed. Neither slept. Starlight glowed through the overhead light tube. When Elly's rhythmic breathing signaled that she was sleeping, Marie said, "What happened with you and her before dinner?"

"I saw her walking off into the woods with some kid."

"Oh, I'm sorry. That's my fault. I didn't see her leave."

"It was probably innocent," said Mike. "They said they were going to see some feral cats ... kittens. But I told her she couldn't go, that she was supposed to ask one of us first."

Marie did not say anything for a few minutes. Then, "She's lonely."

"I know."

"At least at home we could have Lily and Lucy over."

"Yeah," said Mike. Lily and Lucy were neighbor girls a block down from them. Six and eight years of age, they were an odd set of friends for Elly, as she was seven or so years older than them and towered over them. Still, they had been happy playing together.

"How much longer do you think it will take to get to the border?" said Marie.

"I think we can get there by tomorrow night. Or, if we get tired of driving, by the next day."

Marie ran her hand along his arm. "Good. You're a good driver. How hard do you think it's going to be to cross over the border?"

Mike closed his eyes. "I don't know." He tried to sound just the right balance of hope and realism. "There'll be an application process, a wait."

Marie snuggled against him. Mike raised his head to look over at Elly. She was asleep. He pulled Marie closer.

"Sometimes I get really worried, Mike. I worry about her."

"I know. So do I."

"I try to pray but sometimes I can't."

"I know. I'm the same way. Let's put some music on."

"Okay. Not too loud."

"How about the Dylan?"

"Yeah. But skip the first cut, that dance tune."

Mike put the Dylan CD in the player. As the acoustic guitars and harmonica tinkled from the speakers, he pulled Marie close and kissed her. Her tongue went deep and soon they were making quiet, gentle love.

They had a good morning, up shortly after dawn, coffee, some oatmeal. Sitting and watching the day blossom as other campers drove by, waving from their windows. After Mike and Marie loaded up, Elly went inside the camper to sleep some more.

After driving a couple hours or so, Mike finally found a gas station that had gas; the price had tripled since the troubles began. He filled the tank. There was no telling when they would get another chance. They drove for four hours and were discussing pulling over to eat, when they crested a hill and spotted a roadblock a mile or so ahead.

Mike squinted as he studied the vehicle in the distance—a dark green truck, camouflage-painted, straddling the road.

"Should we turn around?" said Marie.

"Probably not. They see us now. They might follow us. Besides, we're going to have to use this road to get north."

Mike drove on slowly. When he was about a city block away, two khaki-clad men left the trees and walked to stand in front of the truck. The younger one had a long gun with a wooden stock slung over his shoulder. Handsome, eighteen or so, he was Mediterranean-looking, with dark hair, wide-set blue eyes, and an honest, non-threatening face. The other, older man had a silver mustache and goatee, and black captain's bars stitched into his camouflage cap. A pistol in a black leather holster hung from his hip.

Mike came to a stop about ten feet away. The two men came up to the driver's side window, the young subordinate hanging back a respectful distance. Mike noticed four more soldiers in the shade of the tree on the left side of the road, all of them with smooth young faces. They watched with mild, bored interest. Mike hoped they were generic local militia, not Minute Men or Liberty League troops.

"Good afternoon, sir," the captain said to Mike. He nodded at Marie. "I'm Captain Moore."

"What's going on?" said Mike.

Moore's face was militarily impassive. "We're not letting anyone through for the next 24 hours. We have information about a force of Liberty League north of us, and a jump jet."

Mike nodded. "Is there any other way up north?"

Moore frowned. "You'd have to go back the way you came, about eighty-five miles. There's a forest service road there you could use to go around."

Mike was not thrilled about going back the way they had come for eighty-five miles, then travelling a gravel or dirt road through the forest.

"You're welcome to stay with us till we clear

43

this up," said Moore. "Shouldn't be more than ten or twelve hours. We have some people checking things out. Should have a report soon."

Mike turned to Marie. "What do you think?"

"It's worth waiting," she said, looking straight ahead, "probably."

Mike turned to Moore. "Well, what outfit are you with?"

"Wisconsin Militia, second battalion, first regiment."

It did not mean anything to Mike, but they did not seem threatening. "Okay. We'll stay for a while."

Moore nodded curtly and stepped back to speak with the young man who hovered nearby. They again approached the truck.

"You'll have to step out to be searched, sir," said Moore. "Sorry, but that's SOP these days. Anyone in the back?"

"My daughter."

"Okay. She'll have to come out and ride with you all in the front."

Mike frowned. They would take his .38. But would they give it back?

Elly walked around to the front of the camper with the blue-eyed young soldier. Mike noted with relief that she was not frightened. She was smiling as she and the youth watched him hand one of the other young soldiers his .38. The young man passed it to Captain Moore.

Moore opened the cylinder, then flipped it closed and carefully put it under his belt. "You'll get it back when you leave."

Mike said nothing. The man seemed honorable. He decided to trust him. What else could he do?

"Why are you carrying that?" said Marie.

"I'll tell you later."

The Captain gave some orders to the men by the tree line. He turned to Mike. "You can get back in."

Mike, Marie, and Elly climbed into the cab of the pickup. The young soldier climbed up onto the running board on Elly's side.

Mike saw that Elly was quite taken with him, her face all lit up. "What's your name," she asked him.

"Gabriel Jilosian," he said with a big smile. "My friends call me Gabe."

"Sir?" said Captain Moore to Mike.

Mike turned to face the captain.

"Private Jilosian will show you the way into the camp."

The young soldier looked at Mike and pointed north. "Sir, there's a turnoff just two hundred feet up on the left."

"Okay," said Mike.

"What's your name again?" Marie said to the soldier.

"Gabriel Jilosian. Call me Gabe."

"Is that Greek?"

The young soldier shook his head and smiled. "Armenian."

"Oh," said Elly. "Are you from around here?"

"Actually, I'm from up near the border. But I've been down here for three months."

Elly nodded in apparent fascination.

Mike kept the truck in first gear as they crept up the highway and then turned off the asphalt. The camper rocked gently as they lumbered slowly down a gravel road. Mike saw the flag flying from a flagpole just above the trees. They drove a bit further and passed through a gate marked by head-high white posts on either side of the road. The camp was laid out in a large circle, with a mowed parade field and flagpole in the center, and a dozen or so manufactured homes equally spaced all around. Camouflaged vehicles, mostly Toyota trucks, with a few ancient-looking Humvees, were parked here and there. As they drove past a double-wide modular building that appeared to be the headquarters, Mike's nostrils picked up the scent of food. Camouflage tarps had been tacked to the roof of one side of the structure and pulled out about thirty feet, then lashed to aluminum tent poles, providing shelter from sun and rain. It was a mess hall of sorts, with picnic tables set up underneath. Mike saw an Asian man looking out of the pick-up window at them as they slowly drove past.

"Pull in here," Gabe called into the window, indicating a square patch of gravel ahead on the right.

Mike turned in and parked.

Gabe jumped down. His feet crunched gravel as he came around to the driver's side. He looked in the window at Mike. "You can stay the night in your rig." He pointed in the direction of the double-wide they had just passed. "The chow hall serves dinner starting at five. Captain Moore wants to talk with you there in the morning at breakfast. He said he'd meet you there at eight."

Mike nodded. "Okay."

"Are you going to be there too?" said Elly.

Marie frowned as Mike said, "Don't bother him, Elly. He has his assigned duties."

Gabe could not hide his interest. "I don't know," he said to Elly. He glanced somewhat apologetically at Mike and Marie. "It's possible." He looked back at Elly. "It depends on my schedule."

"Okay," said Mike. "We'll probably see you around at some point."

Gabe nodded, saying nothing.

"Well, wait," said Marie. "Maybe you could have dinner with us?"

"Hmm," said Mike.

"Sure," said Gabe. "I'll have to go to the HQ and sign in first. What time?"

"Is it opened now?" said Marie.

"Yeah."

"Okay. How about we meet you there in fifteen minutes?"

"Sure."

Elly's smile was radiant as Gabe waved and walked off.

Marie knew that Mike was not happy she had invited Gabe to eat with them, but she did not think there was any harm. Elly was quite taken with him and they would be leaving in a day or so anyway. Marie sat next to Mike on the picnic bench underneath the tarp at the chow hall. Gabe sat across from them next to Elly—their paper plates of hot dogs, macaroni and cheese, and broccoli, before them.

"So," said Marie to Gabe, "where exactly do you live?"

"A town called Littlefalls."

"How big is it?" said Mike.

Gabe smiled. "Tiny. About five hundred people."

Marie watched Elly nodding at Gabe's every word. She was fascinated with the young man, studying him. Mike, however, was reserved, a little uncomfortable with the situation. It annoyed Marie. Couldn't he see the joy in his daughter's face? Wasn't she entitled to be in thrall of a handsome young man like any other young woman?

"How far is Littlefalls from here?" said Mike matter-of-factly.

"About four hundred miles."

"Oh," said Elly, "do you get to go home to see your family?"

Gabe smiled at her and looked around at Marie and Mike, "Actually, I'm planning on going when I get my next leave, which should be in two months."

"Wow," said Elly. Her eyes were bright. Then she frowned. "Are you afraid of this war, Gabe?"

"Nah," said Gabe with bravado.

Mike blinked in thought as he lifted his fork.

"I am," said Elly. "I don't understand it."

Gabe was attentive to her as he chewed.

"Most of us don't, Honey," said Marie.

"It changed everything," said Elly. She looked intently at Gabe. "Do you miss the Internet?"

Mike and Marie smiled.

"Sure," said Gabe. "Everybody does. They still have a military internet, but it's not the same."

Elly's face was somber. "I miss Facebook the most."

They laughed gently.

"I don't," said Mike, "I think we're better off without it."

"Not me," Elly insisted.

"Well," said Marie, "there were some nice things about it, especially in the beginning."

A short while after they had finished eating,

Gabe stood. "I'm going to have to get ready for guard duty," he said.

Marie watched Elly as she watched Gabe walking off and her heart fell a bit. Elly was absolutely taken with him. And what young girl wouldn't be? He was intelligent, mannered, good-looking. Marie tried to dispel the sadness that was rising in her. She'd always worried that her only child might never know the happiness of love and domesticity. And now, with the upheaval in society, was that lost to everyone? And what about her relationship with Mike? He seemed to be changing, becoming more distant and overly suspicious.

In the morning Mike, Marie, and Elly walked in the direction of the headquarters building as the light grew. They passed a couple of houses that appeared empty, then one, in front of which, three young women sat on lawn chairs, one of them holding a squirming toddler in her lap. Hip Hop music thumped through the open windows.

At the chow hall, Captain Moore sat alone under the tarp at one of the tables, a cup of coffee before him, smoking a cigarette. He stood and waved them over.

As they sat, he said, "One of you might want to get your order in for breakfast. Tommy's the cook. I told him your tab was on me. It's just eggs and potatoes, or oatmeal if you're watching your weight." He smiled at Marie.

Marie turned to Mike. "What would you like?"

"Eggs and potatoes, and coffee."

"Okay," said Marie. "Elly, come with me." They went over to the window in the side of the building. Tommy came to the window to take their orders.

"Well," Captain Moore said to Mike as a camouflaged truck rolled slowly around the circular gravel street, "You probably haven't heard the latest."

"What's that?"

"The Liberty League raided dozens of houses in Altoona, Pennsylvania. They smoked a bunch of people that wouldn't turn in their guns."

Mike shook his head. "Wow. That's awful."

Moore nodded, watching Mike closely. "Sure it is. This stuff's only gonna get worse. You might want to consider staying with us for a while."

Mike said nothing.

"There were a couple guys here the day before you."

Mike's pulse quickened. "Riding motorbikes?"

"One bike," said Moore. "A thuggish-looking white kid with a wounded paw and a black guy. Know them?"

Mike realized they must have passed them when they were camped. "I've seen them back in our town," he said guardedly.

"They described someone like you, said they were friends of yours. I didn't buy that. I sure as hell don't buy it now that I've met you and your family."

Mike nodded. "Which way did they head?"

"They went on north. That was before we got word of the jump jet."

Mike tried not to show too much concern. He would have to be on alert from here on out.

"How old are you?" said Moore.

"Sixty."

"That's not too old. We could use you."

Mike shook his head. "I want to get my family to safety first."

Moore's look was sincere. "It's safe here. I could put you and your family up in an apartment."

Mike recalled the three young women sitting

outside the house they had passed earlier. He was pretty sure they were there to service the soldiers. He was uncomfortable with the idea of him and his family spending any more time here. He felt like they would be better off on their own. He shook his head. "No thanks."

"Okay," said Moore. He looked out at the flag stirring in a slight breeze in the little parade field. "But we have to keep the road closed a little while longer. Our assets north of here haven't reported back yet." Moore looked at Mike. "You can head back south towards that forest service road I told you about if you want."

"I think that's what we're gonna do," said Mike.

"Okay." Moore leaned sideways as he reached into his jacket pocket, pulling out Mike's .38. "You can have this back."

"Thanks." Mike, put it in his pocket. He glanced over at Marie and Elly; they were looking into the cook's window.

"So," said Moore, "you're determined to make a run for the border, huh?"

Mike did not care for the "run for the border" wording but kept that to himself. His first responsibility was to protect his wife and daughter. "That's the plan."

Moore blinked, his look turning somber. "Well, you're not alone. Reports are it's getting pretty crowded up there, and chaotic. Were you in the service?"

"Yeah, Syria. I was just a kid. I was in supply and didn't see much action. Mostly just the after-effects ... the bodies. What about you?"

Moore shook his head. "No. Too young to serve. But I got involved with this Militia when the RPP formed and started their campaign. Those people have to be stopped."

Mike said nothing in response. He thanked Marie as she set a paper plate of scrambled eggs and potatoes before him.

Captain Moore got to his feet. "Well, I have work to do. I'll let you all enjoy your breakfast. You all be careful, okay?"

Mike stood and shook his hand. "We will. And thanks for your hospitality."

Moore smiled sadly at Marie and Elly who were setting their plates down on the wooden table. "Goodbye, folks."

They ate quietly, Elly glancing around at

the occasional passers-by. The day had warmed a little and things were quiet when they got back to the camper. Mike assumed most of the men were off on some kind of movement or training; there had been a lot of activity just before sunup, with people walking and talking, vehicles starting up and driving out. They cleaned the camper and got ready to go. Elly asked her mother if she could ride 'shotgun.' Marie agreed and Elly waited for her to get in, before climbing in beside her. She looked around hopefully as they slowly drove the circular road to the gate. Mike knew, of course, who she was looking for, but said nothing. As they came out onto the highway Elly's face darkened.

"What's the matter, Hon," Marie asked, knowing full well what the matter was.

"Aw, I wanted to say good-bye to Gabe."

Mike nodded. "Maybe we'll see him again," he lied.

"Really?" said Elly, brightening.

Marie smiled sadly at Mike but said nothing.

"It's possible," said Mike.

Mike drove south. Soon Marie and Elly were asleep. When his odometer indicated they had driven eighty miles he slowed and searched the wood line on the left carefully. He spotted the turnoff at the 86-mile mark, indicated by a short metal stake in the ground. He slowed further and turned in.

The road was flat and maintained. After a mile or so it came to a fork. Mike cursed under his breath as he stopped. Marie awoke. Moore had not said anything about a fork in the road. Which one was he supposed to take? He took the one on the right.

"You sure this is right?" said Marie.

"Yeah. As sure as eeny meeny miney moe will get you."

They drove for about a half hour until the road came to an end at a deserted ranch of sorts— an old water tower rose above a small, dilapidated house with a caved-in roof and all the windows broken out.

"Shit," said Mike as he stared out at it. "This' sure as hell ain't the right road."

"Well, at least we only wasted an hour or so."

"Yeah. We got another half-hour or so just to get back to the fork."

They were quiet as they drove back, looking out at the thinly forested land on both sides of the road. By the time they arrived at the fork it was already one o'clock. Mike said nothing, turning the truck onto the left fork. They drove on. The paved road continued for the next forty or so miles, then deteriorated into a sandy track. The camper creaked and swayed as Mike negotiated the ruts and scattered rocks and branches lying in the road.

Elly woke. "Where are we?"

"Well," said Mike, "we're still trying to get around the area that was closed off, so we can pick up the main road further north."

Elly stared out at the thin growth on both sides of the truck. "I don't like it here," she said.

Mike said nothing. They drove for another hour and the forest grew thicker, the light more anemic. It was after two.

"How much longer?" said Marie.

"I'm guessing at least four or more hours just to get to the main road above the militia camp."

"That would mean driving this in the dark or camping out here."

"I know," he said.

"Maybe we should just go back to where we were and wait for them to open the road."

"Jeez," said Mike, "we've come this far. Let's just go a little further."

Mike drove for another ten minutes and then

slowed and pulled to the side, bringing the truck to a stop.

"What is it?" said Marie.

Mike pointed ahead. About a quarter mile up the road an old pickup truck was parked. It appeared empty, but it was too far away to be certain. "Maybe someone's there. We can ask them how much farther to get to the main road."

Marie said nothing.

Mike began driving slowly forward. He stopped a couple hundred feet back and left the engine running. "Better let me get out by myself and check it out."

"Okay," said Marie, "be careful."

Mike nodded. "Lock the doors." He walked slowly up the road, looking left and right. He was conscious of the weight of the .38 in his pocket. He heard nothing and there was no sign of anyone. When he was about twenty feet from the pickup, he made out someone's head leaning back against the cab window. He put his hand into his pocket, fondling the .38 as he approached the truck's window. The glass was dirty, and a large spider web hung from the headliner down to the floor of the cab. The man was on the other side of it, as if behind a curtain. Head back, mouth wide open, his cheeks were hollow and the skin on his face yellow. An empty bottle of gin lay on the seat to his right. Mike figured he had washed down some pills with it.

Mike turned and looked briefly around. He did not want to take Marie and Elly any further up this road. It was too remote, too quiet. There was no telling what was ahead. He turned back to the truck, looking closely at the dead man's face. Something dark moved in his mouth—a good sized spider peered out. It seemed to be aware of Mike's scrutiny and backed away into the mouth out of sight.

Mike was about to start back when he heard the putter of a motorcycle engine from around the bend in the road. His pulse picked up and he reached into his pocket to fondle the .38. He heard the bike shift gears as it approached. He heart began pounding. The bike rounded the bend, a middle-aged man giving him an appraising look as he rode past.

Mike composed his expression as he walked back to the camper.

Marie unlocked the door and he got in. "What happened up there?" she said.

Elly watched him closely.

"Just some old guy sitting in there, drunk. He said that the road further up is partly washed out. Who knows if we'll be able to cross it? We should just turn around and head back to the main road."

"Some guy on a motorcycle rode by," said Elly.

"I know."

Marie looked at Mike but said nothing. Mike turned the truck around and started back. After they turned onto the main road, Elly broke the silence with a cheery voice, "Maybe Gabe will be there when we get back."

"Maybe," said Marie, "but it's also possible the road will be open and we can continue north."

"I hope not," said Elly, "I want to stay at the camp again. I want to see Gabe."

Mike had no intention of staying at the camp again and was pleased when Marie gently laughed at Elly's comment. He had already decided to drive slower and give Moore and his men more time to clear the road north. "Yeah," he said, "well, we'll just have to wait and see what happens."

They drove for another hour as the light waned and the temperature began to drop. Mike turned to Marie, "I think we should just find a good place to camp for the night. We'll hit the

Militia check point in the morning or early afternoon. I don't want to get there after dark."

"Yeah, I think you're right."

"Aw," said Elly.

"It's okay, Hon," said Marie.

In the darkness, Mike tamped down their campfire. Sulfurous-smelling steam wafted up, occasionally reaching his nostrils. He tied the chairs and table to the back rack of the rig. Marie and Elly were already in the camper getting ready for sleep. The sky was black, only the brightest stars visible, the rest obscured by low clouds. Mike tugged the rope hard, moving the rig slightly. He turned to look behind him. He was not concerned about animals; it was people that worried him. He saw nothing but comforting blackness and returned to his task. As he reached for the door to the camper, a flash of red in the northern distance caught his eye. It was like lightning, but ruby red. He walked away from the camper out toward the road, clear of the overhanging branches, and looked up. It came again, a thin red line, like tracers, but straight as an arrow, coming from the clouds down to the forest in the distance. He watched a few more moments until it was gone. He went back to the camper and put his hand on the doorknob. He heard Elly talking to her mother. He could tell from her voice she had been crying. He held back a moment to allow Marie time to soothe her. No doubt they had been talking about Elly's attraction to Gabe. Mike felt a familiar pang of sadness. They had almost broken up over Elly. When the extent of her developmental problems became evident, the need to find an explanation had led them to blame each other. Only prayer and sage-like restraint had enabled them to get through that phase. Mike thought of praying again now but could not bring himself to do it. The whole world had gone crazy and God was either indifferent, or off in some other galaxy helping more-deserving creatures. Before climbing into the camper, Mike looked around at the darkened trees once more, wondering what the streak of red light had meant. He went inside.

Things had quieted. He locked the door behind him and got in the bed next to Marie. He fell asleep quickly and slept soundly until the chirping of birds announced the dawn.

They drove slowly north, Mike watching

the odometer. He spotted one of the militia's camouflaged trucks ahead on the side of the road. It pointed off into the woods, as if the driver had not had time to park properly. The driver's door was open. Mike slowed and pulled over behind it.

"I wonder where they are," said Marie as he stepped down on the emergency brake.

"I don't know. Let me check it out and then we'll decide what to do."

Mike got out and shut the door. He heard Elly questioning her mother in a plaintive voice. He walked up the weed-filled slope of the shoulder and peered into the truck. It was empty and the keys were in the ignition. The vehicle did not appear to be damaged in any way. Out of curiosity, he turned the key; nothing happened. He checked to make sure it was in park; it was. Maybe the battery was dead, or it had some kind of electrical short-circuit.

He walked back to the truck. Marie pushed the button, rolling the driver's-side window down. She and Elly leaned toward him.

"It's empty and it seems to have a bad battery or something. I'm going in the camp to see what's up."

Elly turned away from her mother and began to open the door. "I want to go too …"

Marie's voice was sharp. "No. Let Daddy go look. I want you to stay here and keep me company."

Elly's face darkened with frustration. "Okay."

Mike looked at Marie. "I'll be about ten minutes. If someone comes up, just crack the windows, don't unlock the doors."

Marie nodded.

Mike walked up the highway to the turn-off. He walked down the gravel road, coming to the white gateposts. A hundred or so feet away he noticed that the flagpole was gone. There was no wind and his crunching footsteps the only sound as he trod the curving road. He came out into the camp. The buildings were all gone, in their places, rectangular whitish shadows on the ground. Half the vehicles seemed to be missing, and the half that remained were blackened, twisted hulks. He recalled the bright red lines in the sky the night before. So that's what it had been—lasers. He left the road and walked toward the nearest shadow. It was ash, symmetrical, with a few things protruding from underneath, pipes, hunks of concrete, pig-tailed wires, the burnt remains of what looked like a washing machine and dryer. He walked further to where the HQ had been, now a huge rectangle of ash. Twenty feet away, two trucks lay in heat-twisted shapes. He approached and saw just behind them what looked like an ancient sculpture—three men sitting on a log or stone bench. They appeared to be carved from bone or ivory, granular and whitish. Two of them were missing limbs, one had no head. Mike thought of the captain and the young soldier, Gabe, that Elly had been so taken with. Not far away he saw three more mounds of ash—people fleeing? He turned and started walking back toward the gravel road. He paused. The unmistakable remains of a motorcycle lay etched into the earth. It appeared to be a smaller Japanese bike, maybe a Honda. He stared it. There was no way of telling if it was theirs. He started back to Marie and Elly, picking up his pace.

He sighed with relief as he came out of the turn-off and saw them sitting calmly in the truck. He got in and closed the door.

"Well," said Marie, "were they there?"

Mike bit his lip and shook his head. "No. They evidently moved out, the whole bunch of them."

"But I wanted to see Gabe," Elly pouted.

"Just wait, Honey," said Marie. "Maybe we'll run into them further up the road."

"No we won't," said Elly, on the verge of tears.

"It's possible," said Marie. "They have to be somewhere. If we don't run into them before we get to the border, maybe after we cross over, we can come back down and visit sometime. Right, Hon?"

"Maybe," said Mike.

"Really?" said Elly, her voice tinged with suspicion.

"Yeah," said Mike. "But for now, we better keep on going. We have to find a place to spend the night. I don't think we can make the border before it gets dark."

As Mike drove north his mind returned to the burnt-out remnants of the camp. He pictured Moore, Gabe, and the others. He still could not believe people had opted for war so quickly. He remembered the on-line posts, the vicious and cruel comments, mostly, it seemed, young men filled with righteous indignation that anyone would disagree with their fantasies about fighting a war. They were ignorant, without wives and children, most of them. Strong, they could fight or run fast if things went badly. Not so many others. How could people have been so stupid, throwing away the good for the perfect, the utopia? And now what the hell did they have, and who knew where or when it would end? How does anybody turn off something like this once it has started?

And what about him? What had he done or tried to do to stop the rush to this insanity? Not much. He had even waded into a few late-night Facebook insult fests, throwing away all reason and civility while giving vent to his own righteous anger. "But …" a nagging voice whispered in his head, "why not fight?" Neither side was black or white—and he would have to come down on one side eventually. He would. But not until he got his family to safety.

IV

THEY DROVE JUST OVER AN hour before they reached the border. They were about a quarter mile out from the border crossing station when they passed the first vehicle parked on the side of the highway. Another hundred yards up vehicles lined both sides of the road. Some were parked in the trees not far from the road. People could be seen talking beside their rigs or sitting on metal folding chairs around small fires. There were all kinds and types of vehicles—campers, sedans, homemade rigs, even long semis converted to huge campers. The closer Mike got to the crossing station, the more crowded it became, and he realized he would have to turn back to get a place at the end of the line. He made a U-turn in front of a government building, pulled over and double parked twenty feet from the entrance.

"I want to run in and take a look before we go back and park."

Marie nodded tiredly as Elly slept beside her.

Mike walked up to the glass doors. He saw a handful of people inside, a security guard about ten feet away. He tried to push the door open, but it was locked. He noticed the hours stenciled on the glass. Closed at 4:00. It was already twenty minutes past. He put his face close to the glass to get a sense of the place. The security guard saw him and approached. He opened the door and stepped out.

"I just wanted to look around," said Mike.

The guard pointed to a large Quonset hut-type building. "That's where you want to be," he said. "That's where all the action is now… on the Canadian side."

"Really?" said Mike.

The guard went on, "They open at nine, but people begin lining up around seven."

"Thanks," said Mike. He studied the distant building. Through the windows he could see rope lines, a long counter, and in the back about a dozen chest-high cubicles. He went back to the truck.

They were up at seven. Marie made some hot wheat porridge. They had a little pancake syrup to put on it. There was no more saccharin for their coffee.

"We're getting low on pintos, rice, and other

70

things," said Marie. "We'll have to see if we can find some somewhere."

Mike nodded. "We can go after we talk to the people in the station."

"Okay. Hope it goes quick."

Elly's face was hopeful. "Do you think we'll run into Gabe?"

"I don't know," said Mike. "After we talk to the immigration people we can see if there's a local market. If you're out and walking around, you'll see lots of people and it will help you relax."

"Okay," said Elly.

They cleaned up the camper and at 8:00: started up to the border crossing office. The line started in the parking lot on the American side. They took their place, hands in pockets, as the damp cold air clung to them. Mike asked the man in front of them how long he thought it would be before they got in.

The man was in his thirties, with a full frizzy brownish beard. Like most of the people standing about, his face was reddened, his nose running. The man shook his head and smiled stoically. "Yesterday we waited for five hours. Then, when we were almost to the front desk, they closed the place down and made us leave."

"Wow," said Mike.

The man turned away. They waited for two hours, shifting their feet against the persistent cold, staring dull eyed at the trees all around.

"I've had enough," said Marie finally. "I can't stand out here anymore. Let me take Elly and we'll go see if we can find some of the things we need."

Mike looked briefly at the people behind them waiting with bored, resigned faces. "All right." In the other direction, the broad, curved roof of the immigration building was visible, but they were still about a city block away. "They're probably gonna want all of us to be there for the interview. Hopefully today I can at least get us an appointment."

"Okay." Marie turned to Elly. "Come with me. We'll see if we can do a little shopping."

Elly turned to Mike. "Bye Daddy."

"Bye, Elly." Mike felt a familiar pang of sadness as he watched them walk away. He turned around and pulled his collar up. The line shuffled forward about ten feet and stopped.

Mike finally got into the building and to the

reception desk an hour before they were scheduled to close. The woman who spoke to him was tired-looking and officious. He began to explain his situation to her, and she cut him off. "Sir, the whole family has to be here for the interview."

"I understand. I was hoping I could make an appointment for us."

She looked down at her monitor, hit a few keys, and pulled a note pad toward her. "Next Tuesday, the 13th at nine." She swiveled around in her chair and pointed to the rear of the building. "There's a door back there for people with appointments. There's no sign, but you'll see one or two security guards there. Bring all your identification and don't miss this appointment or you'll go to the very bottom of the list."

Mike took his time walking back to the camper. The cold had not abated and there were not many people outdoors. He passed a camper with a small motorbike tied to the rear rack. He thought back to the twisted two-wheeled motorbike wreck at the militia camp. Hopefully, that had been theirs. He passed two men standing between two camping rigs, warming themselves before a fire in a large metal trash can. Heaped on the ground around them were string-tied bundles of firewood selling for five dollars apiece. Mike nodded to one of the men.

"How many?" the man said.

"Just one." Mike did not want to kill himself carrying two of them the quarter mile or so back to the camper, and there was always the possibility of finding cheaper wood for sale along the way. He looped the cord over his shoulder and started toward what would be their home for, hopefully, no more than a couple of weeks.

On the day of their appointment, they walked up the road. Mike realized they had not been this dressed-up since the last time they had gone to church together a couple years back. Marie and Elly wore their overcoats and high leather boots as they walked past the people lined up to get into the building. Passing the point where the line turned into the entrance, a few of the people looked at them suspiciously. They went around to the back. A security guard stood by the door, a bored look on his thirty-something face, "When's your appointment?" he said to Mike.

"Nine."

The man nodded. He cast a quick appraising look at Elly before turning back to look in the window of the door. A few moments later he pulled the door open. "You can go in now."

The same woman was at the counter and waved them over. As they approached, Mike looked around at the lines of people, the workers sitting behind the counters, the two security guards keeping a wary-eyed watch.

The woman gave them a packet. "You'll have to fill all of this out first," she said. "Then come back to me and I'll assign you an interviewer. Do you have all your identifying paperwork with you?"

"Yes," said Mike.

"Okay." The woman pointed to a row of five high tables against the nearest wall. One of them was empty. "You can use that table over there."

A half-hour later Mike, Marie and Elly again stood before the woman. She took their completed forms, looked them over briefly and picked up her phone. "Raza. They're ready." She looked at Mike and Marie. "Just a few minutes."

A tall, heavyset, olive-skinned man in a grey suit came up to them. "I'm Raza Shinde," he said with a smile. "Please come with me."

They followed him to a cubicle in the back of the building. Raza sat behind his desk. Mike,

Marie, and Elly took the three chairs facing the desk.

Raza's face was handsome, with just a touch of excess fat. He opened the folder with their applications, paged quickly through them, then looked up, "I'll go over this at length later. For now, I'd like to ask you some questions."

"Sure," said Mike.

Raza took another quick look at one of the forms in the folder and said, "How was your trek up here? We've been getting reports of fighting not far south."

"Well," said Mike, "fortunately we missed most of it, I guess."

"We stayed one night in a militia camp," said Marie. "They seemed nice." She looked at Mike. "But other than that …"

"And what about you, young lady?" said Raza, leaning slightly toward Elly.

"What?" said Elly in her shy voice. She glanced at her mother for help.

"How was your trip up here?" said Raza.

"Hmm," said Elly in a playful tone. "Okay, I guess."

Raza laughed. "Just okay, huh? What do think about all this fighting, this civil war?"

"What?" Elly again looked to her mother for help. Marie said nothing and Elly looked back at Raza. "I don't know."

Mike said quickly, "We don't talk much about it as a family. It's just something that's going on out there, like bad weather, something we can't do anything about."

Marie nodded in agreement.

"I see," said Raza. He continued to look at Elly. "What do you think about moving to Canada?"

Mike became uncomfortable. Raza's brown eyes were large, and his smile hid something besides bureaucratic interest.

"It's okay," said Elly slowly, looking down at the desk. "I guess."

Raza nodded slowly and thoughtfully like a schoolteacher assessing a student. "Yes," he said.

Raza turned his attention to Mike and Marie. He smiled. "Well, who could ever have imagined we'd see the great United States of America brought so low? And its people lining up to get across the border, like the poor Mexicans used to do?"

Mike seethed inside at the dig but said nothing. Neither did Marie.

Raza took another quick look at a form in front of him. "Okay," he said, "I think everything is in order. You're obviously not drug runners or gang members."

Mike kept his face a blank. Marie smiled politely and Elly made a face.

Raza appeared to have satisfied himself about something or other. He looked at Mike. "I'm going to give you some more documentation that you all will have to fill out." He pushed back slightly from his desk. "We're through for now. I won't need all of you at the follow-up interview, just Mister McNerney."

Mike nodded as they got to their feet.

Raza handed Mike an envelope full of papers. "See the woman you spoke to before," he said. "She'll schedule your follow up interview."

Marie and Elly said goodbye and left the cubicle first. "Thank you," said Mike, reaching out to shake Raza's hand. After getting his appointment slip, he met Marie and Elly outside the back door.

"When is the appointment?" said Marie.

"Two weeks from today, Tuesday at nine."

"Good. He's quite a character, isn't he?"

"Yeah. But we have to deal with him."

"What do you mean, Mommy?" said Elly.

"Oh, only that ... well, there's something odd about him, that's all."

"Yeah," said Elly with a frown.

They started walking and Elly let go of her interest in the subject. "I'm hungry," she said.

Mike and Marie laughed with relief.

"Yeah," said Mike. "Me too." He turned to Marie. "Do we have enough in the larder for a nice big lunch?"

"Yeah, I think we can put something nice together."

They walked slowly down the side of the road toward their camper. Newly arrived refugees drove cars and campers slowly past, turning their heads in search of friends or parking spaces. Mike, Marie, and Elly looked here and there at the vehicles and people on both sides of the road. The temperature had warmed slightly and there was more activity than when they had left for their appointment. People congregated in small groups, turning their heads to look at them as they passed. Some people worked on their camper rigs or puttered about in their little campsites, breaking up firewood, or cooking. Hammering rattled in the afternoon air and they passed a family building a 2x4 and tarpaper lean-to between their smallish car and some pine trees. Mike was struck with the realization that a community of sorts was growing up here before their eyes. He did not like the idea that a lot of these people seemed to expect a long stay. He meant to be across in a couple weeks to a month.

In the morning, Elly announced the snow falling outside with a cry of delight. After they had had breakfast, she went out to play in the snow in their little campsite. All day long it came down. Mike cleared brush away from around the camper and heaped up the bigger limbs for fuel. Inside, Marie washed some of their things in a plastic tub and catalogued what was in their larder, making a list of what they needed. By twilight, the snow was a couple feet deep and still coming down. They ran the heater at fifty degrees most of the night and Mike began to be concerned about the propane. He still did not know where to fill their two tanks.

The next day they made a tour of the campsites on both sides of the road. The snow was wet and clung to their shoes and pant legs as they walked through the confusion of campers and cars and shacks. Mike saw a lanky, young man from behind. Something about him was familiar and menacing. Mike slowed, keeping his eyes on him, until the man sensed his scrutiny and turned. He was not the thug. They continued walking. Half of the people seemed sullen or frightened and deliberately ignored them as they passed. Some nodded in greeting or said hello, and these they stopped to speak with. Elly stood close to her mother as Marie asked a woman a few questions about where to buy food. They walked on, coming to a crew of men digging a trench. Mike looked over at one of them leaning on his shovel as he took a break.

"What's happening?" said Mike.

"Septic trench. We're putting in a dozen two-holers. This place is filling up fast."

"You know anywhere I could buy propane?"

The man's face was serious, even grim, as he shook his head. "Nope. Propane is getting as precious as potable water now. Nobody knows where to get any."

"Okay. Thanks."

They walked on and Mike spotted a familiar old, stake-body truck piled high with used wooden furniture. A brown army tent with a raised, wooden floor was on the other side of the truck. Mike had seen it and the truck when they had arrived and had been meaning to speak to these people. A blue-eyed, craggy-faced old man, his long white hair combed over to cover a bald, pink crown, was attempting to pull a chest of drawers down off the truck. Mike went over, Marie and Elly following him. He helped the man lower the piece to the ground.

"Thank you," said the man with a smile.

"You're welcome."

"My name's, Jake," said the man. "Carlene?" he called into the tent. An older woman, small and thin, but sprightly, with thick glasses and permed brown hair came out. She looked at him expectantly.

"These are our neighbors from the camper on the shoulder."

Carlene nodded to Marie and Elly. "Hello," she said.

"Hello," said Marie, Elly softly echoing her greeting.

Jake turned to Mike. "I meant to walk on down and introduce myself to you, but I got so busy I didn't get around to it yet."

"Don't apologize. I saw your rig up here and I was gonna do the same."

"Would you like to have some coffee and cake?" said Carlene. "I just made some walnut cake this morning."

"We shouldn't impose," said Marie. "It looks like you're both busy."

"It's okay," said Carlene, "We were about ready to take a break anyway."

Jake gestured to a wooden plank table with two stools under it. "Let me get a few more stools."

"And what is your name?" Carlene said to Elly as Marie and Elly sat.

"Elly."

"Oh. Excuse me one minute." Carlene went into the tent.

Marie called after her, "Carlene, I should have offered to help. Anything I can do?"

"No, dear, just relax. I'll be right there."

Mike indicated the chest of drawers to Jake as Carlene brought out the cake and some cups. "You want help putting that in the tent?"

"No. I got it down to work on it. I restore furniture."

Mike nodded. "That sounds like something that's probably in demand nowadays."

"Oh yeah. Hardly anybody buying new. Hardly anything new to be bought. What business are you in?"

Mike frowned. "Well, I'm retired. I worked as an accountant. I'm not sure what I'm going to do when we cross over. Probably any kind of work I can get."

Jake indicated the table. "Sit down and have some coffee and cake."

"This is delicious," Marie said to Mike, pointing with her fork. She turned to Carlene. "Where in Heaven's name did you get walnuts? And sugar?"

Carlene smiled proudly. "Well, I've had the walnuts for over a year. And that's not sugar in the cake, but honey. Jake and I found a farm on the way up here where we bought some."

"Ooh," said Elly as she pushed her empty plate away, "that was so good!"

Marie and Carlene laughed.

"Would you like some more?" said Carlene.

"Sure."

"So," Mike said to Jake, "how long have you been waiting for your papers to cross?"

Jake frowned. "Four, five months now. Feels like time is standing still."

Carlene came out of the tent and set a piece of cake before Elly. Jake turned to her. "How long we been here?"

"About a hundred days." Carlene looked around to see if anyone wanted any more cake. She sat. "We're supposed to be getting our papers soon."

Mike nodded as he sipped his coffee.

"We got one little advantage," Jake added, almost apologetically.

Mike and Marie looked at him.

"Carlene is Canadian."

"Oh," Mike and Marie said together, smiling.

Carlene smiled. "I came down to the States when I was in my twenties. Never thought I'd be going back home to live." She started collecting plates. Marie stood to help.

Mike looked at Carlene. "Are you happy to be going back?"

"Oh no. I loved it in the States. I came down for a job and got married. I never thought of going back home."

"Was that when you two met?" said Marie.

"No," said Carlene. "That was my first marriage."

"And I was married once before as well,"

added Jake. "We've been married twenty years now. Right Carlene?"

Carlene smiled and nodded. Elly picked up a couple plates. Carlene said to her, "That's okay, sweetheart. Your mother and I got it."

Ten minutes later Marie and Carlene finished washing the cups and plates in a plastic tub and put the things away.

"Would you two like to see my beading?" Carlene asked Marie and Elly.

When the women went into the tent, Mike and Jake wandered back over to the chest of drawers, Mike running his hand over it.

"Well," said Jake, "I guess I'll get busy sanding it down."

"You want some help?"

"Sure. Let's see. I got some wire brushes and sandpaper over there. Pull the drawers and you can work on the fronts."

Mike pulled the drawers out and lined them up. He grabbed a wire brush and began vigorously cleaning off a whitish patina that clung to the front of one of them. It felt good to be doing something.

V

M IKE CHECKED IN AT THE reception
counter and waited for Raza to appear.
Not a minute later he showed up in the same suit,
his face shining with bureaucratic can-do. They
shook hands.

As they made their way to his cubicle, Raza
turned and said, "We've gotten a lot of snow,
huh?"

Mike nodded.

"And now this cold. Awful."

"I know," said Mike. "I had to run the heater
most of last night. I have to get in some propane.
Do you know where I can buy some?"

Raza shook his head. "They've been blowing
the refineries up. That's what I hear." He stepped
behind his desk. Mike sat in one of the chairs.

"Well," said Raza, sitting, "let's get down to
business." He leaned forward, folding his hands,
and interlacing his fingers. "I looked over your
paperwork and our data department did as well.
Everything looks legit."

Mike nodded.

"So, I can get your applications in ... probably by the end of the week."

"What happens then?"

Raza leaned back in his chair. "Well, then the big wait begins."

"Big wait?"

"All those people you see out there when you're coming in for your interviews ... They've been waiting, some of them, for more than five months."

"Jesus," said Mike, frowning. "That's not encouraging."

"Sorry to have to tell you that, Mister McNerney, but it's best that you know the reality of the situation." Raza glanced right and left. "You see, the system is completely overwhelmed. There are just too many applicants to process in a timely fashion."

Mike's head filled with all the ramifications of it—the cold, the long wait, their money slowly running out. "God," he said, "that's awful, awful."

Raza leaned back and rubbed his hands together as he looked at Mike sadly. He pursed his lips and leaned forward, his voice softening, "If I could get my superior to sign off on you and your family's application at this office, today, instead of it being sent to Ottawa and sitting there for months, I could probably get the paperwork you would need to cross ready in … two to four weeks."

"How is that possible?" said Mike. "I mean, how do we make that happen?"

Raza leaned forward and lowered his voice, "Well, it's possible, but only if you pay extra."

Mike saw the suggestion of a smile on Raza's lips. A bribe! Of course. And it was not for Raza's superior either, he would be willing to bet.

"How much?"

"Two thousand, five hundred American."

Mike flinched. All their savings had been in their house. They had hurriedly scraped together all the cash they could, but Raza's bribe would leave them with only about seven hundred dollars. He kept his anger and disgust in check, but only barely. "I don't know if I could get that much money together."

Raza nodded sadly.

Mike felt the seconds tick by. "I'll have to talk to my wife. Can you give us some time to respond to this?"

Raza closed the manila folder containing Mike's paperwork. "Sure, Mister McNerney, but not more than a week. When you come back, tell the receptionist that you would like to speak with me."

Mike got to his feet. "Okay."

Raza lowered his head to shuffle some papers on his desk.

Mike walked out.

In the nighttime quiet of the camper, Mike waited till he was sure Elly was asleep before he told Marie everything that had happened.

"We only have about three thousand," said Marie. "That would break us. I knew there was something awful about him."

"Well, you were right. He's a crook. But I'd bet that everybody else who works in there is too."

"We should talk to the Frenchman."

"What? Who the hell is the Frenchman?"

"Anne Marie, a lady who sells used clothes up by the Border Office, told me about him. He's some French guy who sneaks people across the border. For a price, of course."

"C'mon, Marie. Do you really mean to turn our money and lives over to some criminal that's going to sneak us across the border? Do you know how dangerous that is? Think of Elly, if not yourself."

"What else we can do?"

Mike listened again for Elly's steady breathing. He thought he heard a soft voice outside. Probably the people in the next camp. "Well, we could just start the whole process again and insist on a different agent."

"Oh my God, Mike. And add another three or four months to our stay here? We're about to go crazy now as it …"

Mike raised his hand in caution. "Shh. I heard something."

The sound of metal sliding off the fiberglass of the camper shell was unmistakable.

"What the hell?" said Mike. He slipped down from the sleeping shelf, opened the door, and went out. Icy air assaulted him. He saw the dim outline of two people running, disappearing into the haze of blowing snow. His bare feet stung from the frozen ground and he turned back to the camper. The folding chairs and camp table were gone.

Marie's face appeared at the door. "What happened?"

"Well, we don't have camp chairs and a camp table anymore."

"They took them?"

"Yeah, while we were talking." A paroxysm of rage shook Mike. "I'm gonna get dressed and see if I can catch them."

"No, Hon," said Marie. "Don't. We can look tomorrow. And we can tell the authorities too."

Elly's head appeared in the dimness of the door. "What happened? It's cold."

"Get back in bed, Honey," said Marie. "It's nothing. We'll talk about it in the morning."

After Mike secured the camper door from the inside, he climbed up onto the sleeping shelf with Marie. He lay on his back, not saying anything. Marie put a hand on his chest. "Hon," she whispered, "are you okay?"

"Yeah. I guess."

"Okay. I still want to look into the possibility of us paying somebody to take us across."

Mike took her hand. "All right. We'll talk about it tomorrow. Let's try and get some sleep."

Mike went over to Jake and Carlene's place at mid-day. He had promised Jake some help reorganizing the things in his truck. As Mike entered their campsite, Carlene looked up from where she was washing clothes in a plastic pail, purple rubber gloves up to her elbows.

"Hello, Mike," she said, "how's Marie and Elly?"

"They're okay, maybe a little frightened."

Carlene's look turned concerned. "What happened?"

"We were robbed last night, burglarized."

Jake came out of the tent. "I thought I heard some shouting last night. It woke me, but then I heard nothing further and went back to sleep."

Mike nodded and went on with his story. "They got our camp table and chairs."

"Too bad," said Jake.

"Jake," said Carlene, "maybe you could fix them up with a couple pieces."

"Sure," said Jake, "we can find them something."

"I'll pay you," said Mike.

"Don't worry about it," said Jake. He pulled a little .22 caliber automatic pistol from his pants pocket. "You should have one of these."

"I do, but Marie is really nervous about it, so I don't often carry it. I have a little safe in the camper. Anyway, they cut our stuff loose, yanked it down, and ran off with it. I wanted to chase them, but Marie wouldn't have it."

Jake nodded. "We got some stuff you can have. Want some coffee?"

"Nah. Already had mine. We can get to work if you want."

They walked over to the worktable Jake had set up on sawhorses. "I can use you at our place in Canada when you cross over," said Jake.

"Really?"

"Yeah. You don't have any other offers, right?"

"No. We're just focused on crossing over. Figured we'd find something to do once we got there."

"My back's getting worse. I could use your help moving and carrying things, and refinishing. And with your background in accounting … yeah. What do you think, Carlene?"

Carlene was wringing some clothes out by hand. She turned her head. "Yeah. I think that's a good idea. Maybe they could stay in Anne's place out back."

Jake looked at Mike. "Her sister has a house a block from ours, with a little carriage house out back."

Mike frowned thoughtfully. "Wow. That would be a great help to us."

"C'mon," said Jake, "let's get a few more pieces down from the truck."

Mike was getting ready to go up to the border office to speak with Raza when Marie and Elly came into the camper. Elly carried what looked like an Indian basket, crudely woven, the size of a large pot. It had a thin red velvet pillow fitted into its center. Elly set it on her bed.

"What's that?" Mike asked.

"What do you think?"

Mike smiled. "A culturally-authentic pillow for an Indian princess?"

"C'mon, Dad."

Mike laughed. "I don't know, sweetheart. Tell me."

"It's a cat bed. Or a small dog."

"Oh, I see it now."

Marie looked over. "Carlene showed us how to make them. We're going to make them and sell them at Carlene's and Jake's store when we cross over."

"Wow," said Mike. "That's a good idea. It

looks nice, and all the materials you need, except for the pillow, are all around here."

Marie nodded. "Carlene makes the pillows. She has all kinds of fabric and an old treadle-powered Singer sewing machine in their tent."

"Wow, I'm impressed," said Mike. He looked at Marie. "I have to get going. I'm meeting with Raza in a half hour."

Marie looked at him hopefully. "Okay."

Mike walked up the road to the border office with twenty-five hundred dollars in his pants pockets. Fists jammed down on the bills, his head low, eyes alert and wary, his boots crunched on the crusty snow. Once inside the building, he nodded to the receptionist and she picked up the phone. A few moments later Mike followed Raza back to his cubicle. Raza slid his big bulk into his chair and folded his hands benignly. "So, you have talked it over with your wife?"

"Yes. It will really set us back, but we'll pay. We don't want to stay here any longer. This place is getting crowded and ugly."

Raza's look grew somber. "Yes, and that is what I have to talk to you about. Things are changing quickly. Do you know how many people have arrived here in just this last week?"

"No," said Mike, trying to control his growing annoyance. What was Raza leading up to now?

"One hundred and forty-five," said Raza, his face growing more concerned. "Twenty-five hundred dollars is no longer enough. There are people here willing to pay twice that."

Mike could not keep the anger out of his voice. "But you said twenty-five!"

"Please, Mister McNerney." Raza looked out of the opening of the cubicle. "Not so loud."

Mike felt his face flushing. "All we have is the camper, but I don't know how much we'd get for it at this point. I don't even know if we could sell it."

Raza shook his head, the handsome smile back upon his face. "The camper is not all you have, Mister McNerney."

Mike glared at him. "What are you talking about? I already told you. We don't have anything else."

The smile disappeared from Raza's face to be replaced by a look of triumph. "You have the girl."

Mike could not believe what he was hearing.

"Of course I do, she's my daughter. What the hell are you talking about?"

Raza leaned closer, his voice soft and reasonable, "Mister McNerney, come on. I live over five hundred miles away in Toronto. I haven't seen my wife in six months. I haven't been with a woman in all that time, certainly not the dirty whores who are trying to buy their way across. But your daughter … she is a virgin, right?"

Mike said nothing as his eyes bore into Raza's.

"Of course she is," Raza went on, "you and your wife have protected her well. But some man will take her. You already know that. You cannot protect her forever. I would be very gentle with her, and it would only be for one night. Then I will stamp your papers and you can all cross over."

Raza leaned back in his chair.

Mike got to his feet. "Is that it? Are you through?"

"Yes," said Raza.

Mike's face was strained as he walked out. He felt like turning tables over, shouting, throwing punches. As he walked back down the road, he was repulsed by the mess the encampment had become. Trash littered the spaces between the vehicles. The people looked rougher than he remembered when they had first arrived. It was a bad situation and getting worse. When he came up to their camper, Marie was outside raking up the leaves and scraps of paper that had blown onto their campsite. "Where's Elly?" he said.

"She's lying down inside."

He nodded.

Marie paused in her raking. "So, what happened?"

Mike shook his head. "The price has gone up."

"Dear God! How much?"

"Doubled."

Marie turned away from him and began raking angrily. "Well, there has to be something we can do."

Mike said nothing.

She stopped and glared at him. "Aren't you going to say anything?"

"What can I say? We gotta sit down and talk about it. We'll figure something out."

Marie leaned the rake against the camper and went inside. Mike followed her. She was putting her hat on. Elly slept in her bed curled up with her coat on.

"Where are you going?" he said.

"Anne Marie's, the used clothing lady's place. She said the Frenchman is going to be at her camp today. I want to go find out how much it would cost, and other things."

Mike shook his head angrily. "You just won't give up on that, will you?"

Marie shushed him, looking over at Elly. Her face was determined as she turned back to him. "I'm going to find out more about it, that's all."

"Shit," he whispered, "I told you it was dangerous."

Marie said nothing. She pulled her gloves on.

"Okay," said Mike quietly. "Have it your way. Let's go."

Marie pointed to Elly. "We better take her over to Carlene to watch for a little bit."

The light was pale, with a bluish tinge, as Mike and Marie walked past the different rigs, catching the occasional whiff of wood smoke, cigarette, or pipe smoke, hearing a voice here and there. It started snowing when they came to Anne's camp. Used clothing for sale hung from lines all around her site. A woman and man sat before her fire.

Anne smiled a greeting as they came up. She

waved to the man sitting before the fire and he stood and came over.

He was a head shorter than Mike, and small of build, perhaps five years younger. He did not seem threatening.

The man extended his hand, "Bonsoir."

Mike shook his hand. "Good evening."

"This is Julien Bergalt," said Anne.

Julien bowed slightly as he took Marie's hand. "Good to see you. I will help you."

A man and woman entered Anne's site and began looking over the clothes hanging on the lines. Anne went to them and Mike said to Julien, "So, how many people have you helped to cross over?"

Julien nodded effusively. "Beaucoup ... many."

"Well, what's many?"

"Eighteen, no, twenty. Twenty people."

"What does it cost?" said Marie.

"Is it just you two?"

"No," said Mike. "We have a daughter. Three."

A look of concern etched into Julien's thin face as he considered this. "Twenty-five," he said.

Mike laughed. "Well, that's the end of this conversation. We don't have that much money." He looked at Marie. "We should just go."

"Non," said Julien. "Un moment, sil vous plait. Avez vous …"

"We don't speak French," said Mike.

"Uh … have you a car?"

"We have a truck-camper," said Mike.

Julien nodded. "Bon. We could, ah, make a deal, you see?"

Mike shook his head. "No, I don't think so. We're going to need our truck when we cross over."

"No, monsieur, you do not understand. We cannot take the truck over, to cross over. We must go part of the way over on … on the water."

"But I thought it was just a walk straight north," said Mike.

"No. No. There are many police that way. We must, you know, walk part of the way, and then get on a boat and go around. You must leave your truck on this side."

"Well, let's talk about it some more," said Mike.

Marie took Mike's arm. "Hon, I want to go and check on Elly. I'll talk to you when you get back."

Marie turned to Julien, "Goodbye. I must go."

Julien looked surprised. "Oh, that is too bad." He and Mike watched Marie walk off.

Mike turned back to Julien. "All right. Well, I guess we have to discuss how much you'll give me for the truck and camper."

Julien took his hand and shook it vigorously. "Yes, yes. We will talk. First, let us have some coffee, yes?"

When Mike got back to the camper, he found Marie standing outside crying.

"Where's Elly?" he said in alarm.

"She's all right. She's napping again."

"What's the matter? What happened?"

"It's Carlene and Jake. They're leaving in two days."

"Jees! I'm sorry to see them go."

Marie sniffled. "Yeah. Elly's really taken with Carlene. Especially her baking."

They laughed, sweetly sad.

"On the positive side," said Marie, "They gave me all their contact information. They said we could work for them and stay in a little house until we get on our feet."

Mike said nothing. Marie's enthusiasm was

premature. They had no idea what would happen until they actually crossed over.

"So," said Marie, "what did the Frenchman say after I left."

"Why don't we go in? I'll give you all the details."

They sat on their bed, taking care not to make much noise. Marie looked over at Elly, then said softly, "what happened?"

"He wants twenty-five hundred dollars … and the camper."

Marie frowned. "Well, we won't need the camper when we cross over. I told you Jake and Carlene said they have a house we could stay in."

"Damn it, Marie, that's not exactly etched in stone, you know? Without the camper, we'll be on the other side, destitute and without a place to sleep!"

"Oh, so you know that for a fact?"

"I'd bet on it. Why can't you just wait a while? See what develops here."

Marie was red-faced. She glanced over at Elly. "Wait? That's all we do. I'm done waiting. You can stay and wait. I'll take Elly and we'll go."

Mike glared at her, red-faced. He shook

his head. "You're crazy," he hissed. "You're not thinking straight. I'll talk to you later."

Mike left the camper and walked off into the woods to try and cool off. He lamented the fact that their earlier moment of peace and laughter had derailed so quickly into angry argument. But he had to try and dissuade her from this scheme. It was just too damn risky.

VI

MIKE STARTED THE CAMPER AND gripped the wheel. He looked over at Marie and Elly. Today they were crossing over. Elly wore her pink ski coat with white fur collar and a pair of knee-length maroon leather boots. Marie wore a bright blue, puffy down jacket. Mike knew the bright colors were a liability, considering what they were about to embark on, but they had no other options. "So," he said to Marie, "the money is in your bag, right?"

"Yeah. In the envelope."

Mike nodded and pulled slowly out of their spot. He turned to Marie. "I'll bet it won't be five minutes before someone takes our spot."

"Who cares? We don't need it anymore."

"I'm scared, Mommy," said Elly.

"Oh Honey," said Marie. "Don't worry. We're finally on our way."

"I hope so," said Elly.

It was late afternoon. They were to meet Julien and another man who worked for him. Mike drove slowly down the road past the other rigs and cars jammed together close to the trees. "Well," he said, "take a last look. We should be in Canada by tomorrow."

"That's okay," said Marie, "I've seen more than enough of this place."

Mike looked at the encampment in the rearview. Elly said nothing, snuggling close to her mother for warmth and security. They were anxious, Mike knew, and so was he. This deal was a wild, last throw of the dice, and he did not like doing things that way. But Marie had not let it go and had brought it up constantly. Some nights he had used the excuse of having to charge the truck battery to sit down in the cab by himself and listen to the radio. The news was all bad. The fighting had spread across the country. Riots had broken out in California. The last report had Mexican general Cesar Robles crossing over at San Ysidro with his forces to, as he put it, protect vulnerable Mexican Nationals in LA. Other reports indicated that it was they who had been responsible for much of the violence.

Meanwhile, Mike and Marie had continued to argue and finally he had agreed to take up the Frenchman's offer. He had wanted more assurances about him, but what the hell could he do, call the Better Business Bureau?

They drove without talking for about thirty minutes. Mike watched the mile markers. Spotting no. 113, he pulled over and stepped down on the parking brake. He left the key in the ignition as agreed, and they got out. A fire access road cut away to the right just a little ahead. Julien had said that he and his helper would be about an eighth of a mile down the road waiting for them. As they started walking down the snow-packed road, Mike reflexively put his hand in his pocket to feel the reassuring hard surfaces of the .38. He carried a backpack stuffed with everything they could jam into it, and a small suitcase. He thought of what they had had—a house, food and comforts, security, friends—and what they were down to now—a couple of suitcases, a backpack, a .38, and prayers and wishes. Period. But he still had the most important thing, his family. He looked up at the sky. They had a little over an hour before the sun would set.

Marie walked with her bag slung over her left shoulder. Elly clutched her other arm tightly. With Marie's bright blue jacket and hiking boots, and Elly's pink coat with white fur collar and her high maroon boots, they looked like they were going downtown for a night out rather than preparing to sneak across the border into Canada.

They had only been walking ten minutes when they heard some branches snap and Julien came out of the trees with another man. Julien's slight stature contrasted sharply with his companion, who was over six feet and muscle-bound. Mike did not like the setup.

"We go this way," Julien said, nodding in the direction he and his companion had come from. They started walking through forest sparsely populated with fir trees and ferns, stepping carefully over snow-covered logs and rocks. They followed the mottled tracks Julien and his man had left in the snow. The snow was crusted over in places with ice and every now and then Elly broke through, laughing as she grabbed for her mother's arm.

Julien turned around to Mike. "Did you have problems finding this place?"

"No," said Mike. "We've driven this road a couple times before."

"Ah," said Julien, turning back to follow his associate along the trail. Mike followed five feet back, Marie and Elly holding onto each other just behind him.

The big man in the lead stopped and said something in French to Julien. Julien responded, then turned to Mike and said. "We are very close." He gestured. "Just over this hill, on the other side. You must pay the money now."

"Really?" said Mike, suddenly feeling foolish and vulnerable. "I thought we were supposed to pay when we reached the boat?"

Julien again said something in French to his friend. The big man came over to stand beside him. "No," said Julien, "my associate and I have to go back to the road. There are others coming along soon. You must pay now."

"Give me the envelope, Marie," said Mike.

As Marie took her bag from her shoulder Julien shouted, "Maintenant!" He pulled a small knife from his pocket and lunged at Mike. Mike dug his hand into his pocket and pulled out the revolver. He heard Marie and Elly scream. The other man had pushed Marie to the ground and was grabbing her bag. Mike pointed the revolver at Julien, feeling a sting in his other hand as he tried to fend off Julien's slashes and thrusts. He pulled the trigger and the shot boomed through the forest, knocking Julien backwards. He thrashed about on his back, his hands on his belly, screaming in pain. The other man ran off with Marie's bag under his arm. Elly was kneeling over her mother, crying piteously.

He ran to them and knelt to Marie. "Are you okay?"

She nodded in shock. Elly cried and held onto her.

Mike pulled Marie to her feet. "C'mon! You and Elly have to get back to the camper."

Julien's screams made them turn.

Marie looked over at him. "What about him? We can't leave him here like that."

"Damn it, Marie, just go! The son-of-a-bitch who took your bag will come back for him. Maybe I can get our money back."

Marie took Elly's arm and they hurried away.

Mike watched them disappear into the trees. He walked back over to where Julian lay in the moonlight. Mike stood over him. Julien's eyes were closed, and he had stopped moaning, his chest rising and falling slightly.

Mike took the revolver out of his pocket and walked away and up the little rise where Julien's big friend had gone. He stood still, listening.

Only a slight rustle of leaves above reached his ears. Despite what he had told Marie, he did not really think the big man would return. At least not for a while. He walked back over to Julien.

Julien's breathing was shallower. Mike looked up at the moon through the skeletal branches. His mind went back to the sprawl of the camp. They had to go back there now. They had no other choice. And no money, or hardly any.

Mike thought he could smell the camp in the distance. He again wondered if the two motorbike thugs had been at the burnt-up militia camp... if that had been their bike. There was no way of knowing. They could even be back in the stinking, desperate collection of humanity the border camp had become.

He looked down at Julian, then up again at the rise. If only the big man would come creeping back, he could maybe pick him off from behind a tree, get their money back, and put an end to this stupid, sad disaster.

He thought of Marie and Elly sitting in the truck on the side of the road. Maybe the big man was headed there! He had better go.

Marie pulled Elly along. The light was pale,

and they slipped and tripped on unseen, snow-covered rocks and logs. Elly held back and Marie turned to her, "C'mon, Elly. We have to get back to the truck."

"Not that way, Mom," said Elly, pointing, "this way."

Marie looked and saw the mud-smeared broken mess of the snowy trail they had made earlier. They changed directions and hurried on, Marie wondering what they would do now that their money was gone. She felt guilty for having insisted they do this. Mike had been right. Was he okay now? The thought was replaced with the image of the relative safety of the camper and the camp. They all had to get out of these woods and back there. Then they would just have to wait. Surely the situation there would be resolved at some point.

They emerged from the woods onto the logging access road and turned to the right. They slowed their pace a little and a gunshot sounded back in the woods, followed quickly by another. Elly whined in fright.

"It's okay," said Marie. "Daddy will be back in a few minutes, then we'll go back to the camp and try and figure things out. Don't worry."

They walked another couple minutes and Marie spotted the moonlight reflecting off the windshield of the truck.

Coming out onto the road, Mike saw the truck a quarter mile away. A few minutes later he got in. Without saying anything, he started the engine.

As they drove down the highway Marie said, "what happened? I heard two shots."

Mike did not look at her. "The big guy came back with a gun and took a shot at me. I shot back. I don't think I hit him."

As they headed for the encampment, Mike thought about how they were now back to where they had started out, only worse. No plan and now, almost no money. They would just have to take their chances along with everybody else. They rode without talking for a few minutes as Elly continued to sniffle. Mike thought back to Julien. He felt no compassion, no guilt, only anger and frustration.

"She's not hurt, right?" Mike said to Marie.

Marie ignored him, holding tight to Elly as they drove.

"Are you all right, Elly?" said Mike.

"Yeah. I'm just scared."

"Don't worry. We're all a little scared, but we'll be okay now."

Mike's left hand burned from where Julien's blade had stuck him. It was not a deep cut and there was not much blood. Hopefully, it would not get infected. He took stock. They were now out most of their money and were nowhere closer to getting across. And Julien's people might come looking for them. But maybe not. They would just have to lay low. What else could they do?

He glanced at Marie's strained face. She would not look at him. He imagined she was blaming him for all of this. No matter, he told himself. She would get over it.

"I hope so," he muttered aloud, not meaning to.

"What?" said Marie.

"Nothing. Just talking to myself."

The dark and cold pressed against the windows as they drove in silence. It was the end of the line for them. C'mon, he silently told himself. Be positive. Yeah, right.

After a few minutes he turned to Marie again, "I'm sorry it turned out this way."

She glanced at him. She no longer looked

angry, only frightened. "Let's not talk about it right now."

Mike watched the headlight beams probing the black, empty highway ahead. All his imaginings of their lot finally improving had been a fantasy. What in the world was going to happen to them? He stared at the white lines disappearing under the truck, finding no answers. An hour later he drove past their camp spot, now taken by an old van, with two vehicles lined up behind it. He parked behind them and they slept.

Marie seemed to be in shock the next morning. Elly was unusually quiet and furtive. Mike found a half squeezed-out tube of antibiotic cream to smooth over his cut hand. He sipped his coffee and thought of the night before. Marie put some hot wheat cereal in front of him and he ate. A vehicle pulled up on the shoulder outside. The valve tick of the engine filtered into the camper. A door opened and closed. Mike went out, glad for the distraction.

Mike watched as a middle-aged man attempted to back up his pop-up camper with a little Chevy SUV. The camper was blocked by a frozen, hip-high berm of snow the driver could not see.

Mike walked over to the driver. "My name's Mike."

"Elvin," said the man with a mild Southern drawl. He indicated the woman beside him. "This here's Katy, and my boys, Sherman and Bobby in the back."

"You're not clear of that berm back there," said Mike. "Let me go on back and guide you in?"

"Thank you, sir," said Elvin.

Marie and Ellie came out of the camper to see what was happening.

Mike guided Elvin into his spot and a moment later, Elvin and his family got out of the car. Marie and Katy met and seemed to take an immediate liking to each other.

Elly watched with delight as Sherman and Bobby, both about ten years old, immediately began throwing snowballs at each other.

"How'd you come in?" Mike asked Elvin.

"We were west of here, camped in the woods. It was too darn quiet for the wife, though. We heard about this place … and here we are."

"I see," said Mike. "Were you camped in a State Park?"

"No, sir. Just open forest, probably owned by a logging operation. I'll tell you what, there's a place I found just outside of Johnsonville where a man sells all manner of new and used hardware and supplies out of his barn. I wanted to go on back there and take a look. You want to go with me? We can talk."

"Sure," said Mike.

Elvin detached his SUV while Mike spoke with Marie. Then he and Elvin drove off to see if they could find anything useful. As they passed through the crowded section of the encampment near the border station building, Elvin said, "It smells to high heaven around here."

Mike looked at him. "Yeah, there's no proper sewage disposal. When we arrived, there were maybe a couple hundred people here. Now there's a couple thousand. They put in some out-houses, but not enough. People, some of them, have taken to crapping out in the trees. I'm afraid people might start getting sick."

"Well, we're not going to be here long enough for that."

"Yeah? Where you headed?"

"I have a few possibilities," said Elvin cryptically. "But I haven't made my mind up yet."

Mike said nothing. Elvin's comment got him thinking again about his own situation. While he had not completely given up hope, realistically, he did not know what the hell they were going to do.

When they arrived at the barn store, they separated. Mike strolled through the aisles looking at ropes and canvas, old rusting tools, beat-up generators, and propane stoves, all stacked high on tables. There were bins of wire, electrical boxes and outlets and cords, stacks of cut firewood. He had hoped to find a small pot-bellied stove to put inside the camper. Temperatures were dropping and there was a hint of more snow in the air. And worse, they were almost out of propane. Despite asking all over the encampment, there was none to be had. Mike thought that he might be able somehow to pass some of the truck's exhaust through the camper and warm them that way. But the trick was doing it with no leaks. A carbon monoxide leak could kill them.

Mike continued to wander through the various tables for another twenty minutes or so. He bought an old pair of tin shears he thought might come in handy later. He asked the proprietor about small wood stoves and was told that they rarely got them in, and if they did, they went quick.

Mike found Elvin in front of the barn smoking a cigarette.

"You find anything?" said Mike.

Elvin indicated a plastic bag on the ground. "Just a few nicked and dented camp plates and cups."

They got back into Elvin's SUV and started driving back.

After a few minutes Mike said, "Where were you and your family when all this business started?"

"We had a little spread outside Atlanta. But the city went crazy and all kinds of human debris started showing up in the county."

"Yeah. Sounds a lot like our situation as well."

Elvin shook his head angrily. "I never thought I'd live to see the day when a legally-elected president of these United States would be dragged out of the damn White House."

Mike could not stop himself and spat out, "Well, if he hadn't turned into some kind of fucking Nazi dictator, that never would have happened!"

"What the fuck?" said Elvin, turning to glare at Mike.

Mike said nothing, shocked to discover that they were on opposite sides. He should have kept his mouth shut. Now what? He looked out the window. Like many at the time—on both sides—he had thought that historic walkout in the glare of the lights with the cameras running, was unnecessary and demeaning, despite his wanting the man gone. Then both sides had gone crazy and the fighting had started almost immediately. And now there was no end in sight.

"Look," said Mike in a composed and conciliatory tone, "I don't want to get into a long argument about all of that. It happened and I just wish that cooler heads had prevailed, that's all."

"Uh-huh," said Elvin, not turning his head to look at Mike.

They were silent for a while, then Mike said, "Damn! Where are the adults that will show up on the beach to save us from ourselves?"

"What?" said Elvin, annoyance in his voice.

"It's from a famous book, *Lord of the Flies*?"

"Never heard of it."

They fell silent again as they looked out at the cold whiteness of the forest.

"I'm gonna have to be gone tomorrow for most of the day," said Elvin finally. "Could you keep an eye on my wife and kids, and watch no one tries to take our stuff?"

"Sure."

"Thanks."

"Not a problem," said Mike. Despite the now-calm, comradely tone of Elvin's voice, Mike sensed falseness in it. Neither of them could completely distance themselves from their anger and frustration. Neither of them could trust the other. He decided to test it further. "If you don't mind my asking," he said, "where are you going?"

"Ah, I have some people to meet. Gotta see if I can get something set up for us east of here."

Again, the cryptic response. Mike looked out the window. It was partly his fault. If only he had not gotten into politics. "Well," he said, "if you hear about any possibility of getting across, let me know, will you?"

Elvin's response was grudging. "Sure."

They came to the ugly sprawl of the border encampment. The tar paper and blue tarp shanties had spread further out into the woods on both sides of the highway. There was trash and litter everywhere. The authorities had put out 55-gallon drums for trash, but they had quickly filled up and overflowed; the cold winds had done the rest. The piney scent of wood smoke mingled with the unmistakable odor of feces. Both men found the scene depressing and said nothing as they drove through. Five minutes later they pulled off the road and backed up to Elvin's rig.

That night both families cooked a communal dinner over a big cheery fire. Mike and Elvin smoked and talked softly, carefully staying away from the charged arena of politics. Marie and Katy got on well, sharing stories about the beginning of the troubles and their flight, while Elly thrilled in helping and watching over the two little boys.

The next morning Mike, Marie, and Elly awoke to find that Elvin had not simply gone on some mission, but that the entire family had quietly slipped away in the night. The young couple and their little boys had provided a happy, but brief, respite from their recent trouble, and now their isolation and worry returned. That night Mike put his hand on Marie's shoulder, and she turned away from him. As he lay on his back looking up at the darkness he thought again about his and Elvin's argument and wished he had not said anything. After what seemed like a long while he slept.

VII

M IKE WALKED ALONG THE HIGHWAY in the dark. Marie did not like him going out after dark. There were reports of muggings and robberies. But most nights she had little to say to him and read her books sitting up in bed. Afterwards she would go to sleep without a word. The bitter cold had settled in for good and he had started spending his evenings wandering through the encampment as campers cooked outside and talked, hoping for news in general and information about the availability of supplies and propane. This night he had heard little he could use.

He was not far up the road from the camper when he thought he heard something behind him. Before he could turn, someone slammed into him. He landed face-down on the ice-encrusted black top. He could not breathe. His head a swirling rainbow of pain, he became vaguely aware of someone going through his pockets.

In the blackness a male voice said, "You get paid?"

Another voice, closer. "Fuck yeah!"

"What?"

"Fuckin' shit pistol, man."

One of the men laughed and they ran off.

Mike slowly pushed himself to his feet. His side ached almost unbearably. His face stung. Warm blood tickled as it ran down his lip. He put his hand into his pocket. They had taken his .38. He limped back to the camper.

Marie nursed Mike as best she could. The slightest movement unleashed excruciating pain in his side. Marie and he agreed that he probably had a broken rib, but there was no chance of getting a doctor to look at him. Marie did her best to tape his side tightly. He did not bother telling her that his revolver had been stolen. She would not care about it anyway. At least the little money he carried had been safely tucked in his shoe. When Elly saw him the next morning she burst into tears. It took a month for the cut on his lip and his black eyes to heal and fade away.

Pale bluish daylight half-lit the interior of the camper as Mike sketched out his idea for a heating system. Some days the cold stung them, and they wore their coats and hats inside the camper. The propane was just about gone. Marie sat above in their bed, reading. She hardly had anything to say anymore, evidently completely taken over by her disappointment and depression. Elly sensed their unease and was uncharacteristically quiet. She sat on her bed listening to an old Disney CD. Mike looked up at Marie, then down at the sketch before him. He had no training in engineering or mechanics and he knew it was unlikely that he would find the materials and tools needed to craft such a heating device, but the planning and sketching took his mind off their plight. His current scheme involved running the hot gases from the truck's exhaust pipe through a half dozen aluminum or copper tubes with radiating fins welded on. He took another look up at Marie and caught her eye.

"You want to take a walk… the three of us?"

Elly blinked at the sound of his voice. She coughed, but she did not look over at them.

"No, that's okay," said Marie. She too had come down with a cough and cold. "I think I'll take a nap."

Mike felt annoyed but kept the anger out of his voice. "Okay. I'm going out to gather firewood. I'll be back in an hour or so."

Marie said nothing in response.

Mike walked into the woods. He had started staying away from the other campsites as much as possible for fear that one of Julien's acquaintances might recognize him. So far, he had heard nothing and assumed the Frenchman's helper had kept the money and gone off somewhere. Falling asleep at night was difficult. Given the cold, Mike's instinct was to move closer to Marie, but she used the excuse of her cold to keep a distance from him.

Mike searched beneath the grey skeletal trees and dark green firs for firewood. He turned to look back at the camper, visible in the distance. All he had, all he cared about, was back there. If not for that he would head deep into the forest until he dropped.

He walked on, bending to pick up hefty branches here and there, occasionally muttering aloud as he prayed in his head. He was tortured by memories of better times—meals, family get-togethers, movies watched together on the couch, trips to the park with Marie and Elly. He found himself in Gunder's Supermarket. The overhead lights, the colored signs, were vivid, the aisles full of meats, produce, dozens of varieties of pastas and noodles, sauces, soups, rotisserie chickens, wines, beer, cakes, pies… "Fuck!" he muttered.

He heard a footstep and turned. A man and woman foraging nearby had heard him. They turned and disappeared behind some fir trees, their footsteps crunching away.

"I won't let them have her!" he muttered at their retreating backs. He continued searching for firewood. They had to get the hell out of here before their money ran out completely. And if they could not, well, he still had agency. There was one last thing he could do.

"What the fuck am I supposed to do," he muttered angrily to that other, saner, part of his mind. As he reached up to tear a large, rotting limb from a tree, he had a vision of Christ on his cross. "God! I can't see any other way out."

More weeks passed. The encampment grew and their money reserves shrank. One night as Mike lay wide awake, looking up at the ceiling of the camper, Marie's voice came out of the blackness. "So, how long are we going to sit in this awful place and do nothing?"

Mike felt a faint hope. If they could resume talking and regain some of the trust they had

had, maybe they could all get through this. "I don't know," he said. "There are rumors that the Canadian government is gonna let a whole bunch of people in at once. Supposedly some UN observers already came through here. But, like I said, they're just rumors. And there's always talk in the encampment about people sneaking refugees across, but ... that ain't an option for us anymore."

"Well we have to do something. We can't just sit in this camper and freeze to death."

Mike's hope came unmoored and started drifting away. "Of course not, Marie, for God's sake. But we can't do anything rash like before. We have to wait."

"Wait? Why don't you go back and talk to Raza?"

"That wouldn't do us any good."

"Really? Maybe we could make him a deal, give him the rest of the money and the camper."

"He doesn't want the camper."

"How do you know that?"

Mike could not keep the anger out of his voice. "Damn it, Marie ..."

"Not so loud."

He looked over at Elly's sleeping form. He

pictured Raza's oily face and blurted out, "Do you know what he wanted?"

"What? You said he doubled the price."

"No. I lied to you. He wanted something else."

"What are you talking about?"

"Her," Mike said in Marie's direction, "he wanted Elly."

"What?"

Mike saw that she still would not let the thought in. "Look, Marie, the world has damn near completely unraveled." He moved closer to her. "It's turned to shit. I can't help it if you won't face reality, okay? But I'm going to do what I have to do. I'm not going to let him or anybody else end up passing her around."

"What's that supposed to mean?"

"Just what I said, damn it. Without us to protect her, how long do you think she'd last in this new … situation? Look, I'm sorry, but this is the way it is."

Marie turned away from him, saying nothing.

Mike woke at dawn. He got out of the sleeping rack and put his coat on. Marie raised her head to look at him.

"I'm going to see if I can find somebody to take me to the barn store," he said. "I want to hunt for something to make a stove out of."

Marie lay her head back down. "Do what you want. I don't care."

Mike left, stung by her reply. At the barn hardware, he saw a table heaped high with flexible metal tubing. Nearby were packaged rolls of heat-resistant tape. The thought that had been assailing him like a pesky insect came again and he mentally shooed it away, muttering aloud, "No, not that."

Mike and Marie continued to drift further apart. The days grew short and the weather alternated between snow and freezing rain. Despite Mike's angry estrangement from Marie, he worried about her and Elly more than ever. They both had been taken over by the cold and were miserable, coughing frequently. Rumors came through the encampment about distant battles and international intrigue over the border and the refugee situation. Mike busied himself a couple hours a day going further and further into the woods to gather branches for firewood. He managed to fashion a crude stove, but despite his best efforts, it leaked smoke into the camper, and they could only run it for twenty minutes or so before it began to bother them.

Mike and Marie spoke about mundane matters, but she still seemed to harbor resentment toward him. He could not help dwelling on it, forever wondering what he could do to bring her out of it. Short of getting them all safely across the border and into a more livable situation, he could not come up with anything. If he could heat the camper, however, it would alleviate Marie's and Elly's discomfort. But there was no propane to be had anywhere. Raza must have been right about the refineries having been blown up. Fortunately, a gasoline truck came through the encampment on a weekly basis, selling gas by the gallon. He queued with the others with his red plastic five-gallon container in hand.

Mike sat in the cab of the truck, the engine running, "to charge the batteries," he'd tell Marie. But he enjoyed listening to the radio, and guiltily luxuriated in the heat. The big V-6 wasted a lot of heat. If only he could get the right materials, he might be able to capture it and route it into and through the camper. That would improve their lives greatly. But there was always the danger of carbon monoxide poisoning. Hardly a week went by without a report of someone in the encampment dying that way. Some said it was accidental, others suicide. But all seemed to agree—going unconscious and drifting off—it did not seem like such a bad way to go. They had even coined a name for it—camper-cide.

Mike looked out at the trees and the other campers. He pounded his fist on the dash, cracking the vinyl padding. "God! Please! I give up. I can't fix this. Only you can!" Teeth clenched, face pinched, he felt like a child pleading to his father, on the verge of tears. The truck's engine ticked steadily; the heater's blower whirred monotonously. Slowly his anger and frustration subsided, and he found himself feeling foolish and weak. What if Marie were to come out of the camper and see him like this, or Elly? He turned off the engine and walked out into the woods.

Late one afternoon Mike sat inside the camper, reading at the table. Marie lay up in their sleeping rack listening to music through her headphones. Elly had been reading one of her Disney books and now slept.

"Her cold isn't getting any better," Marie said out of the blue.

Mike looked up. She had taken her earphones off.

"I know," he said, at a loss for anything further to say. He had no hope, nothing to offer her. They looked at each other and this time she did not look away. Her eyes filled with tears.

"Maybe we should just pull up stakes and hit the road," he said, "throw the dice one more time. Go south, east, whatever, and see where we land."

She shook her head as tears spilled down her face. "No. You know we can't do that." She sobbed softly. "What are we going to do, Honey?"

He climbed up beside her and held her. They pulled the quilt up over themselves and made love slowly. Afterward Marie slept. As he lay on his back and looked up at the ceiling, he again thought of his scheme. If he could just meter a tenth of the exhaust coming out of the Ford's engine, into the camper, maybe that would be enough to warm it up and help Marie and Elly sleep. But if carbon monoxide got in … Well, it would be the end of all worry and pain. In the anemic light of the camper, a part of him did not have a problem with that. He knew such thoughts were despicable, even evil, but they kept coming back.

VIII

MARIE CRIED SOFTLY IN THE dimness of the camper. Her dream had been so real, she had broken out in tears when dawning consciousness tore her away. Most of the details faded quickly, but the warm house, a table set with good, hot food, and the absence of fear, lingered.

She turned her head. Mike had gone out. She heard a noise outside—someone nailing boards together. She raised her head to look down at Elly. She lay under a mound of blankets and coats, still sleeping, something she did a lot of now. Marie sighed. Her beautiful, little girl, grown up now, but still her little girl. A car drove slowly by outside, then the usual cold quiet settled back down. Marie could not believe they were still stuck here. Mike had lost hope, it seemed. He kept moving, kept planning, kept doing little things, but he and they went nowhere. There had to be something he could do. Or … she could do.

She sat up and pulled the covers off. "Elly, wake up!"

Elly stirred slightly but said nothing.

"Elly," said Marie sharply. "Get up."

One of the coats slid off Elly and onto the floor of the camper as she sat up, blinking her eyes in the dim light. "What?" she said in annoyance.

"We're going out."

"Where?"

"We'll go up to the used clothing lady, and then I want to go talk to Mister Raza about something."

"Okay. Could we try and find some honey or sugar, and nuts too? We could make a cake like Carlene did."

"Yeah. We'll see. Get dressed. We'll have something to eat when we get back."

Later Marie and Elly wandered through the tables of dented and rusted canned goods, assorted chipped plates, cups, flatware, can openers, pots, pans, moldy paperbacks, CDs. Occasionally they ducked under clotheslines hung with shirts, pants, bras, and socks. A block away the steel and glass of the Canadian Border Station took distinct, gleaming shape in the morning sunlight.

Marie turned to see where Elly had gone. It was time to go up and talk to Raza. About ten feet away, a young man had his back to her as he talked with an older woman who held out a folded-up coat to him. There was something familiar about his build and bearing. He turned slightly, not seeing her, and there was no doubt in her mind.

Marie felt someone tugging her arm. It was Elly.

"Mom, it's him!"

IX

MIKE WALKED BACK THROUGH THE encampment with a sack full of things he had gotten at the barn hardware—heat-resistant tape, copper tubing, an antique soldering iron. He had hitched a ride over and back. He was at the end of his rope. They were down to less than three hundred dollars and with the increasing food and fuel prices that would only last them another week or two. Then what? What would happen to Marie and Elly if someone shot him like they did the man four spots down the line the other night? What would happen to him and Marie if Elly's cough got into her lungs? Marie would not survive it. And what would happen to Elly if they were no longer around to take care of and protect her? He had thought of nothing else for weeks. The weight of the tubing and material in his sack gave him some comfort. He still had agency.

As Mike approached their little campsite, he heard a male voice from the other side of the camper. He stopped and listened. Marie laughed softly. He hadn't heard her laugh, it seemed, in six months. Marie's and Elly's voices, happy, carefree, floated on the cold air as they discussed something.

Mike came around the camper and saw them hanging some clothes next to the fire on a line someone had strung there. Gabe Jilosian, the young soldier from Captain Moore's militia, knelt before the fire, breaking up branches into arm-length pieces and stacking them.

"I don't believe it," said Mike, as he set down his sack on the ground next to the back wheel of the camper. "What are you doing here?"

Gabe got to his feet and smiled. He was wearing civilian clothes—jeans, jogging shoes, and a grey woolen coat a couple sizes too big for him.

They shook hands.

"We found him up near that lady that sells used clothes," said Elly cheerfully. "We were like, 'Gabe! What are you doing here?'"

Marie and Elly laughed.

"I told Gabe he could stay with us until he leaves for his folks' place," said Marie.

"Sure," said Mike.

"We're going to put our sweaters on," said Marie. She and Elly went into the camper.

Mike turned back to Gabe. "What happened back there? How did you get here?"

"They got hit. Me and two other guys were out on a patrol. When we got back, we searched the camp. They were all dead, burned up."

"I know," said Mike quickly. He looked over at the camper to make sure Marie and Elly were still out of earshot. "I saw it too. But Marie and Elly didn't. You didn't tell them about it, did you?"

Gabe's wide-set honest blue eyes met Mike's. "Of course not. I just told them I had been given a leave to visit my folks."

"Where are the other two guys?"

"They're on their way home. That's where I was headed. I've been hitching and walking, and when I was passing through here, I saw your wife and Elly."

Mike nodded. "We applied to get into Canada, but the guy that interviewed us wanted a lot of money, more than we had. It's almost impossible to get across."

"There are people that will sneak you across ..."

"I know," Mike interrupted, "we tried that and got robbed."

"My family could get us across."

"Us?"

Gabe's eyes were questioning. "I want to go with you."

"You like Elly, don't you?"

"Of course. Who wouldn't?"

"Well, there are things I have to talk to you about."

Gabe shook his head. "You don't have to go into that. I know she's a little different. That doesn't matter to me."

Mike looked at him sadly. "Okay, well, we'll talk more about that later."

"Thanks," said Gabe. "I think she's really sweet. I would never hurt her."

Mike nodded. Despite all his doubts and fears, he believed the kid. "I know."

Marie and Elly came out of the camper. Marie carried a brown paper bag. "We were able to buy some eggs, some honey, and some other things," she said.

"That's good," said Mike. "I can cook if you want a break."

"That's okay," said Marie, "Elly's going to do it, right?"

Elly smiled. "I hope." She glanced at Gabe then looked at her father. "Mom's been teaching me."

"Well, good," said Mike. "I'll get some more firewood queued up."

Mike felt in shock as he walked around the camper while the others talked. Being suddenly confronted with Gabe and all his youthful enthusiasm and confidence, and the effect he had on Elly and Marie, had been like having cold water splashed in his face. And Elly's innocent and tender love for Gabe was undeniable, a strange, sort-of miracle. Mike picked up the bag of tubing and tape. He cringed at what he had been planning as he quickly put it inside the storage bin, closing and locking the compartment door. He filled his lungs. The cold air carried the smell of frying sausage and he found he had an appetite for the first time in a long time.

Mike went and joined the others. He and Gabe drew closer to the campfire as Elly got ready to flip the eggs in the pan. "Careful now," Mike teased.

Elly turned an egg almost expertly and Mike

and Gabe ooh-ed and ah-ed, smiling at each other like father and son.

"Way to go!" said Gabe.

Mike marveled at the beautiful, happy look on his daughter's face.

"See, Dad," said Elly with a laugh, "I told you I could cook. Mom's been teaching me."

"Well, you certainly can. I guess I can't tease you about that anymore."

Elly's face reflected the golden light of the fire as she slipped two eggs onto a plate her mother extended to her. Marie gave it to Gabe.

After the meal, snow began falling slowly in the dusky light. Mike sipped his coffee next to Marie. They were silent as Gabe and Elly stood together by the road, chatting softly.

"Oh, it's so beautiful," said Elly.

"Yeah," said Gabe. "It would be fun to go sledding."

"Yeah. But we could make a snowman."

"Yeah. Good idea. Let's do it tomorrow morning."

"Okay."

For the first time in months Mike's stomach was full. Marie and Elly had cooked up quite a meal of eggs, grits, and canned sausages. He lay beside Marie on their sleeping rack. Elly was in her single bed down and to his right, Gabe's larger bulk on the left shelf. Mike fell asleep. He dreamed of Elly as a baby. How beautiful she was! Sometimes when he looked into her big bright eyes as he held her, he was overcome with happiness, almost to tears. When they found out about her deficits, they fought a lot, blaming each other, genetics, God, fate, doctors, their friends for trying so hard to be supportive—everyone and everything. What an awful terrible time. But they had come out of it together. And they would come out of this.

Mike came awake. He could hear the steady breathing of the others. He stared straight up, as if he could see through the fiberglass roof of the camper and the low clouds—to the stars. Although the night was as cold as the others, the camper felt warm for the first time in a long time. Contentment washed over him. He turned on his side and slept.

X

MIKE AND GABE QUEUED WITH the others in the darkness of early morning. They each held red plastic gas containers. Cold damp air clung to their clothing as they waited for the fuel truck. Marie and Elly remained back at the camper, packing their things up for their run to Gabe's parent's place.

Gabe lifted his empty container slightly, "So this will be enough to get us to my place?"

Mike nodded. "The truck tank is full. I bought five gallons every time the truck came through and the camper's just been sitting around for the last month or so. This extra gas will be our insurance."

Gabe nodded. They heard a roar in the distance and the people around them came alert. Another roar, closer, a clanging gear shift, and the shimmering lights of a vehicle appeared down the road. A moment later the truck pulled up and stopped with a hiss of its air brakes. The crowd surged forward, Mike and Gabe jostling to keep their place. When their turn came, Mike paid the man and five minutes later they headed back to the camper. The glaring brassy edge of the sun inched over the horizon. Mike felt its warmth on his face and saw it as a good luck omen. They were going to make it.

Mike opened the storage compartment and Elly stepped out from behind the camper. Her face was lit with happiness. "Mom's inside tying everything down." She looked at Gabe. "We're all ready. I can't wait to see your home."

Gabe smiled as he handed his container to Mike. "Yeah, it won't be long. I think we can make it by tonight." Elly nodded as Mike swung the storage compartment door closed and locked it.

Marie climbed down out of the camper, locking the door behind her.

"All secured?" said Mike.

"Yeah, we're ready."

They got into the cab, sitting close together, Marie next to Mike, then Elly, then Gabe. Mike started the engine and tugged the shift lever down into drive. They pulled slowly out of their space. The crowd at the fuel truck had dwindled to a dozen or so men who watched them with suspicious, jealous looks as they passed. No one spoke as they drove by the shabbily dressed migrants and their cars, blue tarp camp shanties, and the occasional column of grey cookfire smoke. Mike turned west at the crossroads and stepped down gently on the gas. The truck slowly picked up speed and Gabe rolled up his window against the inward rush of icy air.

Marie broke the silence. "Well, I'm not going to miss this place."

"Me neither," said Elly dramatically.

Gabe smiled at her, then looked out the window to scan the countryside.

Mike gave Marie a weary smile then turned his eyes back to the road. A half hour later the others slept, leaning up against one another. He gripped the wheel determinedly, keeping the truck in the center of the snowy white road. He thought of what might lie ahead, hoping they had already seen the worst of it.

Marie woke first. She turned to Mike, patting him on the knee. "You okay? Not too tired?"

"I'm fine."

Elly opened her eyes and leaned close to her mother, whispering in her ear. Marie turned to Mike "I think we need to make a rest stop."

Gabe woke and sat up as Mike pulled off the road onto a wide flat snowy stretch of shoulder next to a tangle of skeletal maple trees. They got out of the truck

Marie and Elly walked into a nearby tangled grey copse of bushes and vines, their feet crunching on the crusted snow. In the bright sunlight there was no wind and the temperature had risen above freezing. Mike and Gabe walked across the road into some woods. They were silent as they pissed against a couple of trees. Finishing, they started back, the sound of an airplane in the distance. As their footsteps crunched out of the woods up onto the road, a small, low-flying camouflaged plane glided almost soundlessly over the road a mile or so north of them.

"That's a reconnaissance plane," said Gabe.

"Whose?"

"Probably Liberty League. Captain Moore said they still hadn't found them when he sent me and the others out on patrol. I guess they're still operating around here somewhere."

"Do you think they spotted us?"

"Probably. But I don't think they consider us a threat or else they would have come back around to get a better look."

"Maybe. But just the same, we should get going. You never know."

Marie and Elly talked softly as they came out of the copse of bushes.

"We heard a plane," said Elly.

Mike nodded.

"I wouldn't worry about it," said Gabe. "We're getting close. We'll be there in another couple hours."

"Let's get going," said Mike.

They climbed into the truck and pulled back onto the road.

Mike turned north onto the interstate. An hour later the road took a broad sweeping turn. A large, flat, snow-covered, tree-less expanse showed through the clearing on their right.

"Ooh," said Elly. "That's pretty."

"Yeah," said Gabe. "That's Boulder Lake, frozen over. We're almost there."

"Do you think the river will be frozen over?" said Mike.

"I don't know. Usually it's open. I only remember it freezing over two times and people ice fishing on it. But spring is almost here and the river thaws before the lakes because of the current. I think we'll have open water."

"I can't wait to sleep in a real house again," said Marie.

"Yeah," said Elly. "And when we do, I'm going to keep the thermostat at seventy-five all the time."

Marie and Gabe laughed softly.

The steady reliable drone of the engine encouraged Mike as he drove. After so many days spent doing nothing and waiting, they were finally making progress. Dusk slowly settled over the countryside like a pall. Mike guided the truck down the snow dusted roads as the others leaned back against the seat and cat napped. They came out of the gray skeletal woods and passed pastures and fields blanketed in snow, farmhouses, silos, and outbuildings. Mike turned the radio on and searched for a channel. Static scratched out of the speakers and the others stirred and sat upright.

"Where are we?" said Elly as Marie and Gabe looked about. A collection of buildings came into view in the distance.

"That's Littlefalls ahead," said Gabe.

At the edge of the town they approached an overpass. Just under it, a white van had come to a stop, its red brake lights shining brightly in the dim light. A battered black SUV was parked diagonally in the other lane, effectively blocking all traffic.

"Looks like an accident," said Mike. He pulled up behind the van and they saw a couple dozen people milling about under the stark overhead vapor light. They were all dressed in black. A small gray car pulled up behind the truck, blocking them in. Its headlights went out. On the sidewalk, a heaped-up mound of placarded signs and debris was burning, sending up a column of black smoke. Several men warmed themselves at it. Mike realized with a twinge of panic that it was some kind of anarchist protest.

Two young white men in their twenties came up to Mike's side of the truck and he rolled the window down. The taller of the two had a black woolen cap pulled tightly over his head. His chin was decorated with blue lines and red dots the way some Native Americans tattooed their faces. The other male had carrot-orange dyed hair and a receding hairline. His eyes were like two caverns, darkened with eyeshadow.

"What the fuck are you doing here?" said the tattooed man. "The road is closed."

"We have business in town," said Mike.

The man glared at Mike. His orange-haired partner stuck his face almost into the truck to leer at them.

Mike rolled the window up. The van in front of them drove forward about ten feet and stopped. Before he could take advantage of the space and pull around it, half of the milling mob surrounded the truck. A man in a wheelchair pushed himself in front of their bumper and began banging on the hood with a cane. A slender Ninja-like figure got out of the van and approached. She raised her gloved fist and led the crowd in a chant, "Racist, fascist, homophobe, we're gonna pound you in the road!"

Gabe's face was pinched with anger as Elly looked around in fright. The crowd began pounding on the sides of the camper. Elly held tightly to Gabe as they craned their heads to see what was going on. A solid metallic bang came from the back of the camper. They looked back but could not see what was happening.

The slim, protest leader approached Mike's window. Despite all the commotion and his growing sense of claustrophobia, Mike was struck by her attractiveness. She was young, in her early twenties. Her face had a Hispanic cast--fine, delicately arched eyebrows, dark almond eyes, clear smooth olive skin. But there was an androgynous quality to it that he found off-putting.

Mike rolled down the window. "Will you please tell them to back off and let us through?"

The young woman looked at him with disdain, saying nothing. Mike angrily rolled the window back up. The woman walked around the truck and leaned against it, looking in at the others like a diner in a Chinese restaurant staring into a tank full of fish to choose one for dinner. She pointed at Elly and motioned for her to get out of the truck.

"Ignore her, Elly," said Marie sharply. She turned to Mike. "We have to get out of here!"

"I know. Don't worry. There's gotta be some cops around here somewhere."

The woman moved off into the crowd as they continued chanting in a singsong, dismissive manner, "Racist, fascist, homophobe, we're gonna pound you in the road." They banged loudly on all sides of the truck and camper to keep time. Elly started crying.

Marie grabbed at the wheel. "Just go, Mike. Just go!"

"I can't! That fool in the wheelchair is in the way."

"Just start moving. He'll get out of the way."

"Goddamn it, Marie, I'm not gonna run him over, okay? I just want to get the fuck across the border, not kill anybody!"

Elly looked at him in shock. Mike angrily shoved the shifter up into park.

"What are you doing?" demanded Marie.

Mike ignored her as he opened the door and stepped out. He went to the front of the truck and grabbed the handles on the man's wheelchair and tilted it back.

"Stop!" the man shouted. "Help!"

Mike pulled the chair backward and up onto the curb. He grabbed the man's cane out of his hands and jammed it between the spokes of both wheels. As he started back, he saw Gabe in front of the truck arguing with the two freakish-looking male protesters. The Ninja-like woman came up behind Gabe and said something, distracting him. He turned to her and the tattooed man hit him hard in the face, knocking him down.

Before Mike could get there, Marie and Elly got out of the truck to help. Mike pulled one of the men off Gabe and threw him to the ground.

Turning, he heard Marie scream in anguish. She was rushing at the white van as it pulled away with a screech of its tires. She collapsed in the street, shrieking hysterically.

Mike ran to her.

"They took Elly," she sobbed.

"What?" said Mike.

Marie looked at him aghast and shook her head, continuing to cry.

Gabe came up to them, his face bloodied. "When I managed to break away from the others, that woman and those two freaks were pulling Elly into the van."

They pulled to a stop in the dark in front of Gabe's parent's modest clapboard house. They got out of the truck. Mike and Marie followed Gabe up the walk. He unlocked the door, and they went inside. The place was quiet with only the hall light on. Gabe went into the kitchen and turned the light on. He indicated the table. Mike and Marie sat. Marie started crying softly.

Gabe looked at her sadly. He turned to Mike. "I'm going upstairs to look around. If there was a note or something, they would have put it in the kitchen or else in my room."

Mike waited and said nothing as Marie continued to cry.

Gabe's footsteps came softly down the carpeted stairs and he came into the kitchen. "I don't know where they are. There's no note or anything." He opened the cabinet over the stove, taking down a large can of soup. He handed it to Mike. "Why don't you heat this up for you and Marie. There's some crackers on the top of the fridge there. I want to get something out of the basement."

Mike opened the can and poured the contents into a pot, setting it on the electric element. As it sputtered to life, he found three bowls and spoons, setting them on the table.

Mike heard a tick-tick-tick sound as Gabe wheeled a bicycle into the kitchen. He held a cylindrical bicycle pump in his hand. "I'm going to ride around town and see if I can find the van."

Mike looked at the bike. "You could take the truck."

Gabe shook his head. "No. They would recognize it. I can be a lot more stealthy this way." He pumped both tires up and wheeled the bike to the front door, calling out, "I'll be back in a couple hours."

Mike poured some of the hot soup into two bowls and slid one toward Marie. He noisily opened a packet of crackers and put them on a plate in the middle of the table. Marie looked at the offerings, saying nothing.

Mike sat and spooned some of the soup in his mouth. The crackers were stale. He felt empty inside and ate mechanically. Marie took a few spoons of the soup and then put her spoon down.

Mike sighed heavily. "Look, we'll find her. We won't leave until …"

Marie's chair scraped the wooden floor. She got to her feet without looking at him. She picked up her bowl and spoon and took them to the sink. He heard her spoon out her bowl into the can. Then she took his bowl and spoon. She ran the water in the sink as she washed the bowls.

They sat without touching or speaking on the couch in the dimly lit living room. Minutes or hours passed marked only by the occasional creak of the old house in a wind, a sigh, or a cough. The distinct slap of the gate out front roused them to their feet. Gabe's key scratched in the lock. He opened the door and pushed the bicycle in, cold air following him.

Gabe closed the door and leaned the bike against the wall. "I found them."

"Where?" said Mike and Marie simultaneously.

"They're at an old house on Maple at Sixth. It's painted white with black trim. The van is parked right out in front."

"What about the houses around there?" said Mike, his voice breaking slightly. "Many people around?"

"No. Most of them are empty. I think most of the people have split to their hunting lodges or maybe crossed the border."

"Did your parents leave any guns here?"

Gabe shook his head. "I think I can get in there tonight through the basement garage without being seen."

"No," said Mike. "I'm going in there."

"What are you talking about? There are at least five of them, mostly males …"

"She's my daughter and I'm getting her out of there."

Gabe made no effort to hide the anger in his face as he looked at Mike.

Marie shook her head at Gabe. "Let him go, Gabe."

"He can go in. But I'll be right outside just in case."

The ghostly snow-white streets were deserted as Mike and Gabe walked through the darkened town. Gabe pointed. "We'll cut through here." Their footsteps crunched across a lawn to the back of a house. They peered out. Mike saw the van in front of the house across the street and his pulse started pounding. All the windows in the front were lit and they could hear the thumping beat of Rap or Hip Hop.

"I know this house," said Gabe. "There's a basement entry in the back yard. You can get in that way. C'mon."

They followed the bushes on the perimeter and went to the back yard. They crouched down as they looked at the house in the moonlight.

"You might have to break a window," said Gabe. "After that, I don't know what to tell you."

Mike looked at him. "We'll see what happens."

Gabe nodded. "I'll wait here."

Mike crouched between two dark shadow-like bushes in the back yard. The thump of the music was muted. The rear windows of the house were dim grey squares. Between two black metal railings, a half dozen steps led down to the basement door. He continued to watch. All the action was in the front of the house. He had not seen anyone outside on guard. But that made sense. These people were not trained, disciplined military, just opportunistic amoral thugs.

Mike waited another ten minutes and then moved quickly and quietly across the small patch of lawn, going down the short flight of steps. In the moonlight, the basement door was old and weathered, the knob loose in his hand, but locked. He slid his EBT card between the bolt and the frame and the door opened a crack. It was dark inside. He pushed the door open. Ten feet away another doorway was ajar, dim light glowing from the next room. He approached slowly and paused. The thump of bass was louder as he peered in. The ceiling was low, furniture everywhere, pieces stacked one atop another head-high, with aisles in between. Two ancient-looking big tire bicycles hung from the far wall and beside them a small stairway led up to a door. He heard something aside from the rhythmic bass, an animal-like keening. He went in and crouched down, turning his head to locate the sound. It came from the vicinity of one of the wooden support posts. He headed for it and saw Elly sprawled on the floor, her hair hanging over her face as she cried. Her arms were tied around the post.

Elly gasped as he came up and he put his finger to his lips. She closed her eyes as he whispered in her ear, "Don't worry. Don't talk." He took his penknife out of his pocket and started sawing at the rope securing her to the post. There were half a dozen loops of clothesline and he had cut through half of them when he heard the door open at the top of the stairs. It was the androgynous-looking young woman, the leader. She was holding a bowl of food or water. As she turned to close the door, Mike folded the penknife and backed away behind some stacked bureau drawers.

The woman's footsteps clumped down the stairs and across the wooden flooring. Mike watched her kneel beside Elly and put the bowl on the floor. If she saw ... the others would be running down here. It would be over. He heard the soft mutter of her voice and Elly's sniffling reply.

He got into a crouch and approached. Elly's eyes went big at sight of him and the young woman started to turn. He had to keep her quiet.

He put his arm around her neck and his hand over her mouth. He pulled her backward and down onto the floor. She fought but he was stronger. As she struggled, he felt her small soft breasts under his arm. Her struggling slowed as if she wanted to communicate something to him. He relaxed his grip slightly and she renewed her struggle wildly, whipping her head about. His hand slipped off her mouth and she got out a low cry. He grabbed his left wrist and pulled his arm tightly around her neck, cutting off her air. Her struggling became panicked, and he wrapped his legs around her to keep her from kicking. He leaned back, pulling on his wrist as hard as he could.

He came to consciousness as if he had blacked out. His arm was numb, the girl a warm, sweaty dead weight on his chest. He sloughed her off and crawled over to Elly. "Shh, shh, shh," he repeated as he sawed the remaining ropes. Taking her hand, he led her out through the basement door. They crossed the lawn and went into the darkened bushes. When Elly saw Gabe, she rushed to him. They walked hurriedly without talking. When they got back to the house, Gabe said to Mike, "You better put the truck in the back."

They sat around the kitchen table by the light of a single candle and ate more of the soup and crackers. Then Marie and Elly hurriedly gathered up the bowls and spoons and pots and washed them as Mike and Gabe went out to the back to get the truck ready. Marie and Elly left the house and Gabe locked the door. They got into the truck without speaking. With the headlights off, Mike pulled out and carefully drove the three blocks to Main Street.

"Go left here," said Gabe as Elly snuggled kitten-like against him. She had not left his side after they had taken her from the house and had slept cuddled on the couch beside him as Mike and Marie slept nearby on padded recliners.

Mike drove slowly, hunched forward, as he strained to see in the dimness. Marie and Elly still had not broken their silence. They passed out of the town proper and into farmland. The morning light grew slowly revealing a line of trees where the river flowed to the north.

"Slow down," said Gabe, sitting up. Elly sighed and looked out the window. Gabe pointed. "The turn is coming up. Here!"

Mike made a right down a long snow-covered gravel driveway to a small farmhouse. The neighboring property was still wooded, a long rectangular expanse of twisted bare, grey branches rising out of the snowy ground. They parked next to the farmhouse and Mike saw a small boat house a couple hundred feet away. They got out of the truck.

"Let me make sure they're gone," said Gabe as he headed for the door of the farmhouse. Elly followed him as Mike and Marie stood looking after them. Gabe tried the door, then knocked. After a few moments he and Elly walked back.

"Nothing, huh?" said Mike.

"No. Let's go."

They walked the path down to the boat house, their feet crunching on the snow and gravel. The river came into view--a thousand or so feet wide, mostly open, dark greyish blue with moving lines and ripples as it rolled by.

The boat house appeared big enough for several boats. A black tarp hung down in front. Gabe untied it and tugged it open. A small rowboat lolled gently in the rippling water. "They took their big boat," he said. "Looks like we're gonna have to row."

"Elly," said Marie, "get in the boat."

Gabe held Elly's hand as she climbed into the boat and took a seat in the rear. Marie followed her.

Mike caught a blur of movement back toward the house. The white van pulled up. Its headlights went out. "They're here," he said, "at the house."

Elly started whimpering in fear. Marie put her arm around her.

Gabe untied the boat. "Get in, Mike. I'll pull us out."

Mike climbed in and put the oars in the locks as Gabe began towing the boat out of the boathouse. A volley of shots rang out and he fell onto the concrete.

Mike got to his feet, the boat wobbling. "Are you all right?"

Gabe sat up. "I don't know. Just help me in."

Mike pulled the boat close and Gabe slid down into the prow. They heard voices approaching.

"C'mon," said Gabe, "They're coming!" He leaned down to look at his leg.

Mike pulled hard on the oars, sending the little boat out into the flow. Another volley of gunfire erupted, several rounds rattling into the boathouse. Mike pulled as hard as he could, the strokes whipsawing their heads as the boat glided out into cold bright light. A single shot rang out, sending up a small geyser of water six feet away. Mike pulled frantically, one of the oars breaking the surface and splashing the others. The current took hold of them, moving them swiftly sideways down-river, putting them behind the trees and out of sight of their attackers. The shooting continued but grew sporadic and faint-sounding.

Mike called to Marie, "Check on Gabe."

Marie started crawling forward.

"No," said Gabe, "I'm all right."

Marie sat back.

Gabe pulled up his pantleg. "It's not bad, I don't think. It looks like a welt."

"It's bleeding," said Marie.

"Yeah, but not too much."

They were mid-river, drifting swiftly. No one spoke as Mike continued to pull for the other shore.

"You want me to take over?" said Gabe.

"No." Mike craned his head around, spotting an opening along the icy shore--a bank of black gravel and brown earth, with patches of crusted snow. He headed for it. A few minutes later the prow scratched up onto the gravel, the aft end of the boat swinging out slightly. Mike got out and pulled the boat up further. The others climbed out carefully, talking in low voices.

Mike walked off into the shade of some nearby trees. He brushed the powdery snow off the gray trunk of a downed tree and sat. Marie, Elly, and Gabe remained near the boat. He heard their soft talk, a small burst of gentle laughter. He felt leaden, exhausted. He closed his eyes and remembered the girl's softness against his chest, her panicked, then unconscious, convulsive movements. Confused and empty of feeling, he let his head hang down. Someone put a hand on his shoulder. It was Marie. "Elly told me what happened."

He nodded, saying nothing.

"Look at them. They're so happy."

Mike looked over at Gabe and Elly. They held hands as they looked across the water at America. He shook his head sadly. "I can't believe what I've done."

"You did what you had to do."

"Yeah," he said softly.

"Do you think they'll come after us?"

He sighed heavily. "No. But we better get going." He stood uneasily, checking his footing on the icy rock and stones. "Where's the info

Jake and Carlene gave you with their address and everything?"

"In my bag back in the boat."

"Okay. Let's take a look at it."

Marie put her arm around his waist, and they walked over to Gabe and Elly.

Thank you for your purchase of *Crossing Over*.
Please take a look at Paul Clayton's other works:

White Seed: The Untold Story of the Lost Colony of Roanoke
What really happened to the lost colony?

Calling Crow (The Southeast Series Book 1)
1555. Calling Crow is haunted by his recurring dream of the Destroyer who will one day lay waste to his village.

Flight of the Crow (The Southeast Series Book 2)
Calling Crow travels down the Southeast coast in search of his wife, Juana, taken by the Spanish.

Calling Crow Nation (The Southeast Series Book 3)
Calling Crow faces the most difficult challenge to his judgment and leadership yet, as the hostile Timucua, who have allied themselves with the Spanish to get the deadly thundersticks, move north in search of more slaves and conquest.

In the Shape of a Man
At 1015 Crestview, little seven-year-old
Reynaldo cowers under the escalating
abuse hurled by an adoptive mother

Strange Worlds
Traditional sci-fi/fantasy and satire. Clayton
channels the spirits of Huxley, Orwell, and
Philip K. Dick in these and ten other intelligent,
provocative, and highly entertaining stories.

Van Ripplewink: You Can't Go Home Again
In 2015, a backhoe at a construction site in
Philadelphia unearths a coffin containing
the long-slumbering Van Ripplewink, who
went into the ground 49 years earlier at age
17… Van attempts to make sense of the
new world in which he finds himself.

Carl Melcher Goes to Vietnam
2001 Frankfurt eBook Award Finalist: The year
is 1968. Like thousands of other American boys,
Carl Melcher is drafted and sent to Vietnam.

Talk to a Real, Live Girl and Other Stories
Traditional sci-fi/fantasy and satire. A space miner finds the company of female robots unfulfilling and longs for a real girl. However, there's only one on Kratos and she's taken. A couple goes to Mars after buying a house at the new development there, Happy Acres. Their bliss is cut short when the almost-exterminated shabugalugs make a stealthy comeback.